The Meltese Dodo

A hardboiled planet with a fever, hired by a desperate species to "get something" on The Environment, doesn't want to believe that the beautiful species itself could be the guilty party.

To Winnie & Bob

Michael Hurwicz

Irthlingz

POB 969

Eastsound, WA

The publisher offers special discounts on bulk orders of this book. For information please contact:

Irthlingz
POB 969
Eastsound, WA 98245

First Edition
Printed in the United States of America

The text of this book is set in 12 point Courier New.

ISBN: 978-0-9656989-2-4

I.

I was just getting into what should have been the cooling down side of one of those 100,000 year cycles. You know: Every year, you tilt your head a little farther away from the sun and feel that tingle as the ice inches down the back of your neck, like a conspiracy of twelve-toed Plutonian creep-frogs.

It's okay. You start off as a fiery swirl of gas, and it seems like you barely cool down to molten rock before they bury you under ice. Then you get smacked with this heavy, humid tropical heat that makes you wish one of those dinosaurs or pterodactyls would hurry up and invent lemonade or iced coffee. Then it's another ice age.

You gotta have a split personality to do this job. It never quits, and there's nothing to be done about it. You spin on your axis, wobbling a little in my case (old Big Bang injury). Every now and then, you need a change, you reverse your magnetic polarity.

Then Evie rings through.

"There's a *Homo sapiens* here to see you."

"A what? A customer?" I say, sighing.

"I think so," she says, "but you'd want to see it, anyway. Nice-looking, know what I mean?"

"Well, all right, show 'em in." I haven't been feeling great lately, think I may have a little fever. Wouldn't mind a day with a good book and my feet up on the desk. (I'm in the middle of Dashiell Hammett's *The Maltese Falcon* - for the third time.) But I listen to everyone. Sometimes there's something that needs fixing and you happen to be the one that's meant to fix it.

So this species ambles in. And the temperature in the room goes up four degrees. (Or is that just me?) Holds out its hand. Opposable thumb. Ape family. But balancing on its hind legs, no tail and not much hair. Looks vaguely familiar. And yet, somehow, like something I've never seen before.

Introduces itself: *Homo sapiens*. One of those smoky voices: The kind of smoke you get when a perfume factory burns down on the dark side of Venus. Or a field of night-blooming orchid cactus (*Epiphyllum*) catches fire at midnight on a new moon.

Homo sapiens. The name echoes through the caverns of my memory like a half-forgotten song that maybe brought a tear or a smile back in the day. *Homo sapiens*. Can't place it. But, look, when you're 4.6 billion years old, you're happy if you can remember what direction to orbit in.

"Can I help you?" I ask.

"I hope so." It's a long story, but the gist of it is this: There's this evil genius psycho mass serial killer - calls himself The Environment - who strikes out of nowhere, eventually murders 99.9% of all species with tsunamis, tidal waves, typhoons, diseases, droughts, famine, floods, heat waves, cold snaps, hurricanes, dust storms; and always eludes capture.

"Yeah. I know him. Masterminded that big hurricane down south. Rough customer."

"Well, The Environment is back," says HS. "Someone's been putting the heat on him, and he's coming after me for it." And the species launches into this long string of "natural" disasters, homicidal weather, and freak occurrences that should happen once every million years or something, and now we're seeing them every other weekend, like clueless in-laws. And every time, coincidentally, *Homo sapiens* gets jacked up one way or another.

"Yeah? Well, that's the way the baby bounces."

"You think I'm crazy. I thought I was going crazy, too. Then I got this note."

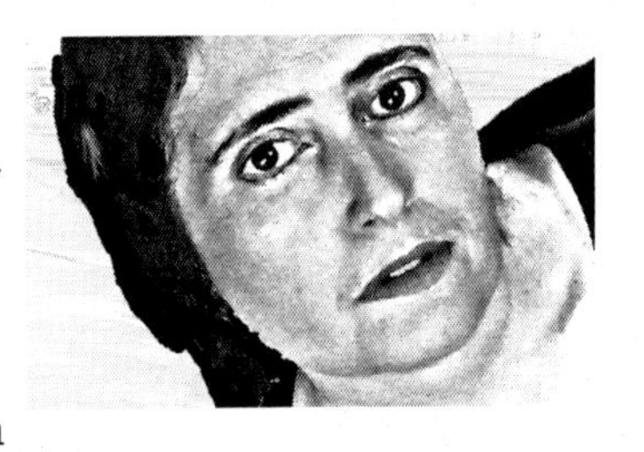

Hands me something that looks like it's etched in stone, carved in wood, worn away by oceans, rivers and rains of untold ancient time:

I have the Meltese Dodo. Do not attempt to separate it from me. TE.

"So? What do you want me to do about it?"

"I need to get something on The Environment. Something that'll give me the upper hand."

And I'm thinking - *This one smells* ... "You want to go up against The Environment?" … *like methane meandering up through melting Alaskan tundra.* "And you want my help?"

"I have nowhere else to turn," it begs, its eyes glistening with something that could be tears.

Like a flaming flock of Mercurian mudslappers feasting on ringtailed rot-rats.

"Please!" it sobs.

Enough to curl your nose hairs into a bow-tie.

"You've got to help me."

"All right, all right. Enough with the waterworks."

"Thank you! Thank you! But, uh ... do you work alone?"

I can tell it's worried I can't handle this by myself, so I say, "No, I got a partner."

"Because, The Environment is big. Real big."

"Don't I know it. But my partner, they call him The Extinctor. You want to talk about coming out of nowhere? When this guy gets through with you, you'll have to hike a hundred light years just to get back to nowhere. We been working together since I could remember. Not a big talker. But a big doer."

And all this time, I'm hearing a little voice - *Watch yourself. This one could blow back on you like a Saturnian night special semi-automatic with a dirty slider and over-sized ammo jammed in backwards.*

Then *Homo sapiens* reaches into its pocketbook and lays all this green on me.

"You going to call your partner?" it says.

"Gotta do some leg work first. Talk to some species."

"Like ...?"

"Reliable sources. Life forms I've known for millions of years. On the down and dirty. Bacteria. Yeasts. Molds. Guys like that."

It looks at me like I'm nuts.

"Perhaps," I say, "you're not familiar with the work of Bonnie Bassler, the scientist who showed not only that almost all bacteria can communicate, but that they do, all the time? Real quiet."

"Really? But do they live long enough to actually have anything to talk about?"

"In Kalaallit Nunaat, Greenland, these dormant bacteria (*Chryseobacterium greenlandensis*) hauled up from two miles down in 120,000 year old ice have been revived. And bacteria can live in my permafrost for half a million years, and in my sediments, amber, and halite for millions of years."

"I guess you would know."

"I guess I would. Talk about an itch. Man! Now give me a couple centuries. I'll get back to you."

"I don't think I have centuries," it says, rubbing its jaw nervously.

I just look at it. I work on my schedule. Nobody hurries me.

"I've already let this go too long. Fifty years. We have to turn it around now. That's what the wise guys say. Otherwise ... I'm toast."

I shove the green back at it. I'm pretty sure it's not going to pick it up.

It just looks at me. "See what you can do. Please."

Big, sparkling, sad, intelligent eyes. Full of imagination, love, poetry. The kind of species you'd hate to lose. (Then again, I miss them big, bumbling, nutty brontosauruses, too.)

"Well ..."

"Please."

And I'm thinking - *Maybe that smell is just sweat.*

"I'll come with you. I'll help."

It's got plenty to sweat about.

"Nah. Too dangerous. Besides, you'd just be in the way. But I'll pound some pavement, see if I can kick up any dirt."

hup!

II.

So, after a prolonged period of pavement-pounding, I'm parlez-vousing with this sand flea (*Talitrus saltator*) on the beach at Cannes. (Hey, just because you're a hardboiled detective don't mean you can't enjoy yourself once in a while. Besides, I shed plenty of shoe leather getting here, and I'm working.)

The flea tells me rumor on the rue is someone's putting the heat on The Environment, and TE's hitting back - hard. Somebody oughta do something about it.

"Look, I'm working the case, but I gotta know everything before I make my move. What kind of heat are we talking about?"

"Hup!" says the *T. saltator*, leaping across the arugula salad, "Hip! You want to know everything about heat and The Environment? Two words: Hop! Joseph Fourier. A truly great scientist! Hup!"

I think that's more than two - even if you don't count the Hip-Hop-Hups.

"Fourier … Fourier …" I pop a juicy chunk of papaya in my mouth, eyes closed against the sunlight filtering through the blue and white striped umbrella. Adjust the chaise longue one more notch towards the horizontal. The black beret a smidgen more down the forehead.

"Fourier … Rings some kind of a bell -" Maybe in a distant church tower, calling monks to supper in a French Napoleonic provincial village?

Perhaps another shot of that papaya schnapps would jog my memory. I feel with my right hand for the bucket of ice on the little white table. But then something starts to come to me. Vaguely, but … "Wasn't he a ..."

"A Homo sapiens?" says Homo sapiens.

"Yes!" I say. Then my eyes pop open. "*Homo sapiens*?! Hey! What are you doing here? I thought I told you it was too dangerous."

"Oh, yes, I can see that. A real battlefront assignment. Speaking of which, where's your partner?"

"Ah, he's around here somewhere."

"Care for some dressing?" *Homo sapiens* asks the sand flea.

"*Si'l vous plaît.*"

It shpritzes the flea's salad with oil, then vinegar. Replaces the two little squarish bottles in the stainless steel holder on the table.

"He was a *Homo sapiens*! I knew I recognized the species! Why, you're brilliant!" I say to *Homo sapiens*. "One of the few species who ever really tried to understand me."

"Well, we are known for that," *Homo sapiens* admits shyly.

"Don't be modest!" says the sand flea. "Why, he was one of the greatest scientists who ever lived! The father of modern engineering. And the Hup! author of *Analytical Theory of Heat*."

"Ooh! Look! Isn't it beautiful!" trills *Homo sapiens*, looking towards the ocean.

Just underneath the surface of the darkening water writhes a pulsating purple-pink trail, miles across. Here and there, the liquid fingers of the waves stir amethyst sparks.

Homo sapiens starts slipping off her high-heels.

"Yeah! I remember now," I say to the sand flea. "What a pal! Really wanted to understand. And then somehow, we lost track of each other. I'd love to look him up. What was the name of that town again?"

"He was born in Hup! Auxerre. And he Hop! died in Paris."

Dead.

This kind of thing is why I have to get out of the business. And it's the reason I can't get off this merry-go-round. Otherwise, the bad guys win. Death wins.

"How'd he die?"

"I believe he fell down the stairs."

"Right. Fell. Or … had a little help."

"But, why ..."

"Maybe his theory of heat was a little too hot for someone's comfort? And that someone decided to cool it off - permanently."

"But his work is the foundation for all modern engineering," says the *T. saltator*.

"I'll do a little nosing around, see what I can sniff out."

"The trail's a little cold: He died in 1830."

"You call that cold? I remember a missing person case in the Neolithic. Hikers found that misper 5300 years later sticking out of a melting glacier. Now there's a cold case."

Down by the shore, *Homo sapiens*, extending her delicate, slender ankle, puts a toe in the water.

"Watch Hup! out for the ..."

Her foot disappears in a wave.

"... Stingers! Hundreds of *Homo sapiens* have been Hup! stung."

(Hundreds? Wouldn't you think after the first few, the rest would get wise?)

Homo sapiens' foot must be just inches from undulating jellyfish tentacles.

"The stings cause burns which can provoke asthma in humans," drawls a loggerhead turtle (*Caretta caretta*), fore-flippers swooping gracefully, like slow wings, as it gobbles up a jellyfish. "But I love'em ..."

"Perhaps you better say something to her," says the flea.

I don't know. Maybe she needs to learn a lesson.

"She is *Homo sapiens*, like your friend, Fourier. You should protect her."

I jump up.

"Hey, dollface! You heard the flea!"

"I don't know if they do hear us," says the flea.

"Stingers!" I shout.

"Mauve Stingers," says the flea. "*Pelagia noctiluca*, the nightlight of the sea. There must be Hup! Hup! millions of them out there."

"*Homo sapiens* even get allergic attacks, and in rare cases, maybe a little heart failure," continues the turtle, selecting another jellyfish for dessert. "Me, I just wish I had a Tums now and then." It swallows the dessert Stinger, and follows up with a beautiful bass burp.

Homo sapiens pulls her foot back out of the water just as a lone luminescent phantom launches out towards it from the glowing watery trail, a four-inch translucent parachute with eight thread-like stinging tentacles floating six feet behind it.

"Mi-i-llll-ionnnssss," says the *P. noctiluca*, its voice ghostly, echoey. "S'won-n-derful! Lo-ots of frien-nds. Never-r get ho-omesick for A-a-frica."

"You came all the way from Africa?"

"And boy are my tentacles tired! Ha ha!"

Homo sapiens lopes away from the water.

"Hey! I'm sorry," says the stinger. "I thought it was funny."

"I wonder where she's going?" I ask no one in particular, as *Homo sapiens* disappears in the distance. "You don't think she might … get into some kind of trouble up there?"

"Don't worry," says the flea. "Nothing up that way but hotsy-totsy hotels, ritzy restaurants and swanky shops."

"Great. Maybe she'll stay there for a while ..."

"Probably," says the flea. "I've noticed that humans can take a long time to admit they can't afford the 1200 Euro cashmere-and-chinchilla sweater and settle for the ten Euro cup of coffee. Speaking of which, I think I'll forage for some organic debris now. Hup! Hup! Hip! Hop!"

It starts hip-hopping away down the beach.

"Wait a minute!" I shout. "Who was the last person to see Fourier alive? Did anyone stand to benefit by his death? Do you know anything about the Meltese Dodo?"

"The what?" asks the sand flea.

H*omo sapiens* comes back in a hotsy totsy ritzy swanky Cannes bikini and runs into an extra big wave, back out screaming, tears in its eyes, drops into a chair, yelling, "Help! Water!" and rubbing her legs, which are covered with raised strawberry red welts and bits of clinging jellyfish tentacle.

"So-orry!" says the stinger, "But I don't stick my feet in your face."

"Don't rub it!" squeaks the sand flea. "And no water! Schnapps! And fresh papaya!"

"What?" I ask. Can't believe my ears. The flea seems to want to cover *Homo sapiens* with refreshments.

"Water and rubbing make the tentacles discharge more poison. Alcohol or vinegar stops the poison. And papaya enzyme breaks down the toxins."

"Vinegar?!" protests *Homo sapiens*. "I'm not a salad!"

So I use the schnapps.

"And some ice for the pain," adds the flea. "You have a handkerchief?"

"Sure." I fill my hanky with ice from the bucket and, kneeling, apply the compress to the welts.

"Ahhhh." *Homo sapiens* looks down at me, again with those eyes. "Mmm. Thank you. I feel so ... stupid."

"Well, you smell … great … like papaya and schnapps."

"Thank you. That's so much better." She pats my receding hairline.

Suddenly, I'm feeling very unprofessional. I put the hanky in her hand and jump to my feet. "Forget it. You owe me a bottle of schnapps."

"Half a bottle," she says, holding the hanky to her leg.

"Three quarters. On ice." I turn to the Mauve stingers. "Why'd you have to do that? You got something against *Homo sapiens*?"

"No-o! In fa-act, we lo-ove them for getting rid of these vi-icious turtles and tu-una. Soon, it will be just like the go-ood o-old da-ays: jellyfish, plankton, and bacte-eri-ia. We're ge-etting clo-ose alre-eady. Co-ome o-on i-in and se-ee," suggests the jellyfish, flickering electric reddish-blue in response to a wave. "The wa-ater's wa-armmmm! Ni-ice."

"No time. On a case. Thought I had a lead there for a minute," I say sadly. "An old pal of mine. Joe Fourier. But I guess someone got to him before I did."

The jelly ingests some algae, then says thoughtfully. "Joseph Fourier? Tha-at is to-oo ba-ad. Perhaps the mo-ost influ-uential mathematical physicist of all ti-ime. His *Théorie* is a cla-assic."

"*Ah, oui*! Joseph Fourier! The daddy-o of modern engineering!" says a *Streptococcus cremoris* bacteria, having overheard our conversation during a pause in the improvisational trumpet solo it was playing with a cool French beatnik bebop jazz quartet in an intimate club on a slice of cheddar cheese on the plate on the little round table.

Reverentially, the goateed poet bacteria who is improvising with them removes its beret and clutches the hip bit of black fabric to its heart. "The cat who wrote *Analytical Theory of Heat*? The first to realize that your atmosphere acts as a blanket, slowing down the rate at which your heat evaporates into space? *Quel génie*!"

"Ho-ow do yo-ou bacteria know so-o mu-uch?" asks the jelly.

The poet *S. cremoris* shrugs Frenchily. "*Je sais pas*. We're a cultured life form, man." Then it adds, flexing its spherical cell wall dramatically for emphasis, "He showed it was possible, through what is now known as 'Fourier analysis', to take any flow of heat, no matter how chaotic it might appear ..."

The trumpet player raises its instrument to its lips, and the band improvises a seemingly chaotic moment of abstract impressionist sound-painting, while the poet declaims something about "bass blue bangs up against piano-key black and white smashes into saxophone silver trips over trumpet gold bumps bongo brown."

Then sudden silence.

"... to take any flow of heat, no matter how chaotic it might appear," the poet continues, "and mathematically describe it as a combination of smooth, regular, predictable wave forms, like the purest of musical tones. One single, golden trump of the trumpet. One solid silver tone from the saxophone."

The trumpet and saxophone follow the poetry musically. And poetry follows music as the piano-man bacteria strikes and holds one key and the bass-man bacteria plucks a final grounded growl.

"Through this insight," says the poet, his arms describing dramatic arcs in the air, "complexities of heat transfer that had eluded understanding for centuries were resolved to an underlying order of stunning elegance and simplicity, much like that of harmonic resonances. Fourier showed how heat flows, dances, walks through walls - vibrates, y'know - like music. For those who were hip to it, Fourier seemed to have written out - in a few crisp, clean equations - the score for the music of the spheres."

"Maybe," I say, "somebody didn't want to face that music, and decided to settle the score - forever."

"*Eh ou-ais*," says the trumpet player, doubtfully. "In any case, he felt that the most important application of his new theories would be understanding your heat budget: how the sun warms you and how you lose heat through radiation back into space."

"Hmm. A heat budget."

"*Oui*. How much you take in, how much goes out – like a budget."

"And maybe somebody don't like living on a budget, and decides to bust the piggy bank!"

"Ri-ight. Now, anyone who starts thinking about how the sun warms you encounters a strange fact: As you go higher, closer to the sun, you'd think it'd get hotter; but no, the temperature goes down. So we find permanent snow on top of high mountains. And lower down – farther from the sun – you have baking deserts in places like Death Valley and the Great Basin. It's the same pattern nearly everywhere, at all times of year, throughout history and prehistory."

"Wait a minute. Doesn't hot air rise?"

"Yet it's cold up high, hot down below. It's a kick in the head, *n'est-ce pas*?"

"Yeah. But … I know Sol is the source of my heat. I can feel it. Where the sun shines, I get warmer. I'm gonna ask Sol about this some time."

"No need," says the *S. cremoris*: "It's warmer closer to your surface because, although the sun is the source of the light, you are the source of the heat."

"Me? I guess that's possible. My core is like a million degrees."

"If ten thousand is like a million, yes. And Fourier knew your core was hot. He deduced it from the fact that temperatures rise the deeper you drill down into your mantle. Also, anyone who knows about volcanoes can guess that there are some very hot places deep inside you. However,

Fourier also knew that your core heat had almost no effect at your surface, and therefore almost no effect on your atmosphere."

"How did he know that?"

"He had done a lot of studying on how spheres cool."

"Joe didn't get out much, did he?"

"Towards the end of his life, he was so weakened by rheumatism that he had to have a wooden box built to hold him up while he worked. Only his head and his arms poked out of the box. But his thinking was still outside the box. He had figured out the precise mathematical relationship between how quickly it warms as you go towards the center of a sphere, and how much internal heat is being lost at the surface of the sphere. So if you could shove a thermometer way down into the earth ..."

"Oo!"

"Sorry, man. What I meant is, if, in some entirely pain-free fashion, one could measure the temperature gradient going down through your various levels - crust, mantle, outer core, inner core - you'd see relatively gradual warming. That proves - and Fourier knew that it proves - that you are now radiating very little of your internal heat at your surface."

"But … you said I'm the source of the heat."

"That's right. But it's not your own internal heat that warms your surface. Fourier concluded that visible light coming from the sun slips right through your atmosphere, doesn't lose much of its energy on the way in, and doesn't heat your atmosphere. But when sunlight hits you, some of it is converted, Fourier said, into '*chaleur obscure*' - dark heat - which then radiates from your surface, and which your atmosphere prevents from escaping."

"Dark heat." I laugh, perhaps not too respectfully. "That sounds pretty weird."

The little fella takes a deep breath, then lets out kind of a fluttering sound. Speaking to the jelly now, but for my edification, the bacteria says:

"Our estimable ball of dirt feels that one of the most outstanding mathematicians and theoretical physicists *la France* - no man, the world - has ever produced sounds weird. That our Joseph, who stands with Galileo, Newton, Maxwell, Planck and Einstein as one of that select group who, thanks to the originality and influence of their work ..."

It's frothing a bit, all over what I assume would be its chin, if bacteria had chins. It's not pretty.

I'm sure it's right, though: There's plenty I don't know. And, I have a feeling, plenty I'm going to learn.

III.

"*Notre Joseph* was one of the most brilliant mite feeders who ever lived! He penned mathematical odes to you, spinning them out I might say like great wings that took him high above these narrow, winding streets, these half-timbered houses, even above the spires of this great gray edifice with its magnificent stone arches, glorious stained glass windows and 15th-century clock, out to the sun, the planets, the stars, into past and future times so distant they could be glimpsed only through the lenses of poetry or mathematics."

After banging my bean on Joseph's famous treatise (and definitely deciding to stick with this detective/planet gig rather than trying to get into the mathematical physicist racket), I'm getting chummy with this dust mite (*Dermatophagoides pteronyssinus*) up in Auxerre, Joseph's home town, and it's swearing on a Bible (slightly dusty) that Joseph was loved and respected by everyone.

"Right." I pull my beret down towards my left eye. "And now he's dead. Convenient, ain't it? Dead men solve no differential equations. I'm thinking maybe someone didn't like the slope of Joseph's graph and decided to substitute an infinite series – the easy way. Did he have any enemies? Did he mention a Meltese Dodo?"

Just then, a church mouse scampers by, carrying a piece of cheese.

Homo sapiens screams, "Eek! It's a mouse! Run! Kill it! Get the traps! Call out the cats!"

"What's the matter with the mite feeder?" asks the *D. pteronyssinus*.

I just shrug and pat *Homo sapiens*' shoulder. "There, there, dear." She calms down some.

"You'd think the mouse had long green fangs and breathed fire," says the *D. pteronyssinus*.

Homo sapiens disappears, leaving the mouse contentedly nibbling its creamy morsel of Camembert.

"She's just a little … sensitive," I explain. "*Homo sapiens*, you know. Very brilliant. But like I was saying ..."

"Right. Enemies." The dust mite shrugs contemplatively. "During the revolution the Jacobins were going to guillotine him a couple of times for speaking out against their corruption, but ..."

"Sounds like a rough bunch. I'll need to talk to 'em."

"*Désolé*: They're all dead, too."

Looks like somebody's trying pretty hard to close this case prematurely.

"I understand Joseph may have stumbled onto something - possibly a sinister super-villain - known as 'Dark Heat.' And just maybe," I add, "stumbled into some serious - perhaps deadly - heat from parties as yet unknown."

"Yes. *Chaleur obscure*. That was William Herschel's discovery, actually," says the dust mite.

Herschel … Herschel. The name seems familiar. Did Sol mention him to me? Mental note - *Talk to William Herschel.*

"But Fourier," says the mite, "seems to be the first mite-feeder to conclude that your atmosphere must play a key role in keeping you warm. In his *Memoir on the temperature of the earth and planetary spaces* he illustrated how he thought this worked by describing an experiment conducted by Swiss physicist Horace-Bénédict de Saussure.

"Saussure started by lining the interior of a wooden box with black cork, to absorb and hold heat. Then he inserted three thin panes of glass into the cork, spaced about an inch and a half apart, like glass shelves inside the box. He put a thermometer in the bottom of box and in each of the spaces between the panes of glass. Finally,

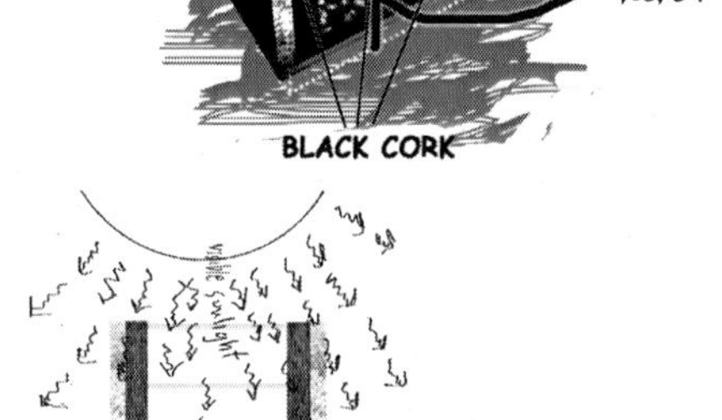

he sealed the box and the spaces between the panes of glass, so no air could escape.

"When he exposed this apparatus to the sun, the thermometer in the bottom of the box showed the highest temperature, and each thermometer going up showed a progressively lower temperature. Fourier asked, why is that? When you think about it, why wouldn't it be the other way around? Why wouldn't the thermometer in the bottom of the box, furthest from the sunlight and shielded by more panes of glass, be cooler?"

I scratch my beret. "You know, the universe is always pulling stunts like this, but I never get used to it."

"Fourier had a theory about how it worked: He said that once light hit the black cork in the box, it was converted into *chaleur obscure* and had difficulty getting back through the glass. Most of it was trapped. And he said your atmosphere, like glass, is largely transparent to incoming visible sunlight but opaque to *chaleur obscure*, trapping heat near your surface."

"Easy to get in. Hard to get out. Just like trouble. The question is, who are the troublemakers?"

"Troublemakers? I would try the English!" says the mite. "Do you know, they boil kidneys! Boiling. Steaming. I tell you in two words: James Watt. The steam engine. There, I believe, you will find the root of all your troubles with heat and The Environment."

If that's two words, I'm the center of the universe. But I get the feeling the climate here might not be real healthy for me, anyway: Anyone around here even remotely connected with this case seems to have ended up on a slab.

"I'm back!" announces *Homo sapiens* brightly. Her arms are full of yowling cats, clickity-clackety mouse traps, and green poison pellets.

"I think she's just maybe a little ..." I begin, but the mouse has already scurried into the shadows, leaving the cheese behind.

"Crazy?" says the dust mite.

"I was gonna say nervous. C'mon, doll, let's get outta here." As I escort her towards the high, shadowy triple arches of the front entryway, I try to explain to her, eight different ways from Sunday, that she's making the informants nervous and she's gotta get rid of the anti-mousery and amscray-blow-get-lost-dangle-drift-dust-sneak-go-home. She seems to understand.

"If you're going to England," calls out a *Penicillium camemberti* on the mouse's cheese, "let me give you the name of a yeast I know. Really into heat."

London
Auxerre

IV.

After a few days of playing footsie with the concrete, I'm doffing my black top hat to the lively little yeast in question, and trying to explain about France and Fourier and Herschel and *chaleur obscure*. Maybe it's just the heat in the kitchen (the oven is set to 175 degrees Centigrade), but the little guy is practically percolating with enthusiasm, fermenting briskly in rich brown dough, bubbly with carbon dioxide.

"Hmm. It's awfully brown," says *Homo sapiens*.

"What?!"

"The flour. It's awf ..."

"What are you doing here? Didn't I tell you to … "

"Amscray? Blow? Get lost? Dangle? Drift? Dust? Sneak? Go-home? As a matter of fact, you did. But I'm very adaptable. Pretty much at home anywhere, from tropical jungle to the arctic." Then, she takes my hand, like I was her mama or something. "Besides, I can't be alone now. I need you to protect me from The Environment. Sometimes I think you don't care if I live or die!"

"You mean I got options?"

She laughs like I was kidding. Then she looks at the bread pan with the rising dough, and the bag of Purely's Organic Whole Wheat Flour on the counter next to it. "Hey, you know what's really good? You remove all the brown parts and you spray the flour with chlorine dioxide gas to make it nice and white. Then you add sugar and vitamins and it's enriched. Enriched," she repeats, turning the word over lovingly on her tongue, like a trigger man fondling a new bean-shooter before a big job.

"But is that really good ..." the yeast begins. It has a high piping voice that makes it sound like it's excited all the time.

"And you hardly have to chew it at all. And, maybe," *Homo sapiens* continues, "instead of adding the sugar and vitamins, we can genetically modify the wheat so that ..."

"*Homo sapiens*, you know," I whisper to the yeast. "Just like Fourier. They're real smart."

"Yes. Herschel was *Homo sapiens*, too," says the yeast.

"Yeah, Herschel. Tell me about him."

"And we could genetically modify the yeast!" says *Homo sapiens*.

"Get her out of here!" the yeast whispers urgently.

"Imagine yeast with fingers, so it could knead the dough itself …"

"Get her out of here!" the yeast yells.

"That's swell, swell!" I say to *Homo sapiens*, patting her shoulder. "Why don't you go get some of that chlorine die-off-cide gas like you said?"

"Chlorine dioxide gas."

"Yeah, some of that, and just everything we need to really do the job right."

And out the kitchen window (which we came in through) she goes, with a tiny little gentle bit of help from my right foot.

"Take your time," I tell her. Then to the yeast: "Okay, let's make this quick."

"So you were there?" the little guy bubbles, loosening up now that she's gone. "Brilliant, brilliant! France! Fourier! If only I could have lived to ..." It grows wistful for a moment, then continues effervescently, "Can you imagine what it must have been like when Fourier confirmed Herschel's discovery - this strange, invisible *chaleur obscure* - and then applied it to ..."

"Whoa! Back up! Who is this Herschel? I got a feeling Sol mentioned him to me. How does he fit into all this? What was his last known address?"

"William Herschel. Local boy." It nods towards the kitchen window, which looks out on the prosperous, bustling town of Slough, a few minutes west of London. "An amateur astronomer. Herschel observed a curious phenomenon having to do with light. Invisible light, to be precise."

Invisible light. Now, why would this mug want light to be invisible? Unless he had something to hide! "Did this Herschel ever mention a Meltese Dodo?"

"Not that I know of. But when Fourier found out about Herschel's discovery, he realized it helped explain how your atmosphere keeps you warm."

"Yeah? Go on."

"William - whose day job was music (he played oboe, cello and organ) - also had a wild, obsessive passion for astronomy. He built a series of telescopes, each one bigger than the last. Eventually, he built a 40 foot scope."

I don't see where this is going, but you can't hurry a yeast. You just have to trust that when you need them, they'll rise to the occasion.

"Among other things, William observed the sun. He put dark glass filters on his telescope so the sun wouldn't damage his eyes. He found that some filters let through a lot of light but almost no heat. With others - the red filter, for instance - he felt a lot of heat, though most of the visible light was blocked. Herschel decided to test all the colors of the spectrum to see how much heat they produced.

"Yeah! I remember now. Sol said they used to play these games together. Good times."

"Though a bit dangerous," added the yeast seriously. "This arrangement worked for Herschel, who must have been very skilled, or very lucky, or both. But don't try it at home. You risk burning your retina, and possibly blinding yourself permanently. And the intense heat could fry your eyepiece."

I get the feeling Herschel must have really wanted to understand Sol, the way Fourier wanted to understand me: Not just the obvious stuff.

"Herschel," the yeast continues, "set up an experiment where sunlight passed through a slit and then through a prism (which he borrowed from a chandelier), producing a rainbow of colors on his table. Then he positioned three thermometers on the table, painted black to absorb as much heat as possible. One thermometer he placed in a particular band of light, the other two just beyond the light - or so he thought! -- on either side to measure

the temperature of the air in the room, for comparison.

"And here's what was amazing, and what Fourier based his theory on: The thermometer just below the red end of the spectrum - apparently completely outside the rainbow of light - actually registered a higher temperature than either of the others!"

"Wait a minute, the thermometer was outside of the rainbow of light, but it heated up 'cause nothing was shining on it?"

"As contradictory and impossible as it seemed, Herschel reasoned, there must be an invisible form of light below the red band!"

- *Invisible light … Right. Reminds me of that old canned dehydrated water scam.*

"He named this form of light 'ultra-red' - beyond red."

Homo sapiens bursts into the room (through the window), with sifters, beakers, test tubes, bunsen burners, white cloth bags stamped "potassium chlorate," frosted plastic bottles labelled "sulfuric acid."

"Uh, maybe we better be going now." I try to lead her back out the window. The result: She sets up her thingy near the window. Sifts the whole wheat flour, tosses the bran and wheat germ into the garbage.

"They're very experimental," I say to the yeast. "Like Herschel." I take her arm. "Come along, dear." But she ignores me, all into pouring something that looks like gin over some white powder.

"You see," she says, "just pour a little sulfuric acid on some potassium chlorate, and you get chlorine dioxide gas."

A door opens in the next room.

"Well," says the yeast, lightly, "time for us to pop into the oven. Oh, by the way, that Watt bloke you asked about earlier. He invented the steam engine. Not English, though. Scottish, sure as my name's *Saccharomyces cerevisiae*!"

I'm thinking - What kind of parents give their kid a name like that?

"By the way," I say, "sounds to me like this Herschel may be a material witness. I'd like to take a statement from him." Actually, I'd just love to meet the guy.

"What do you mean? He died in 1822."

"Aha!"

"Of natural causes."

"Natural causes. Anything like the 'natural' disasters that roughed up my client?"

"Herschel was 83 years old."

"Don't think I'm just gonna let this go. Herschel was a pal of Sol's, and Sol is a pal of mine."

Amid the sound of approaching footsteps from the next room, a freshly budded yeast pipes up, "What's a steam engine?"

I head for the window, *Homo sapiens* trailing behind me, looking back longingly at her mad science experiment, as the older yeast explains, "A steam engine uses boiling water to produce steam that moves a mechanism, which performs work."

And even as we hear the groaning of the oven door, and the metallic clank which can only mean someone thrusting the bread pan into the open maw of death, the sprightly old yeast is telling the youngster about the industrial revolution, machine-based manufacturing, mechanization of the textile industry, iron-making and the increased use of refined coal.

I call out my thanks to the yeast - but I'm not sure if it hears me before the ominous "thunk" of the oven door, followed closely by the roar of *Homo sapiens'* experiment going up in billowing clouds of floury smoke.

* * *

Cars and buses go by as I brush scorched flour off the front of my suit.

"So, let me get this straight," I say, bending down to pick up my top hat, "after you enrich it like this, you eat it? How do you do that?"

"They're omnivorous," says a passing airborne *Pseudomonas syringae* bacteria. "They can eat anything."

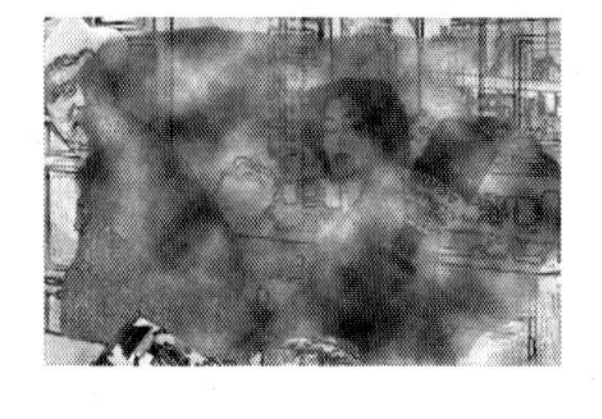

Homo sapiens brushes cindery ash off the back of my head and shrugs.

Herschel. Another one gone. I guess maybe someone is trying to send me a message. Well, I got a message for them: I'm not quitting.

Still, right now I feel like a lone interstellar traveler blasted by obscure invisible dark light in a scorched cosmic flour-dust storm.

Well, guess I'll check out this James Watt.

"That sounded pretty interesting," says *Homo sapiens*. "Using boiling water to produce steam that moves a mechanism, which performs work."

"Yeah," I say, brushing a flurry of blackened flour dust out of my hair.

"We could use something like that to pump water out of coal mines. That way, we could burn more coal to boil more water ..."

"Listen, hon, maybe you ought to go … somewhere far away … and wait for me. I'm afraid you're gonna hurt yourself." Or kill the both of us.

"I'm okay. I'm fine."

I'm afraid she really believes that.

V.

We beat feet northward into Scotland. All the way, *Homo sapiens* can't stop talking about her great idea.

"Yeah, yeah, yeah, okay," I say, finally. "Why don't you go to school and learn how to do that? Read some books, draw some diagrams. Come back and we'll form a committee and discuss."

She runs off into the distance, like a puppy chasing a butterfly. You gotta give it to *Homo sapiens* for enthusiasm. It's really a very appealing quality.

A few minutes later, I'm telling my story on a drizzly hilltop on Eaglesham Moor, a couple hops from Glasgow, Scotland, and tipping my hat - my plaid Scottish Glengarry cap, with three black ribbons hanging down the back - in the direction of a shaggy, brownish-gray hare. It stops chewing its bit of brownish-purple scenery, twitches its flat, dark snoot.

"Your wee yeastie was close to correct," allows the *Pseudomonas azotogensis* bacteria playing (extremely) miniature golf on the bit of root in the rabbit's mouth. "James didna invent the coal-fired steam engine. But he made fundamental improvements in its design."

"The yeast did mention coal," I say.

"Strange, is it not?" marvels the bacteria, taking a number one wood out of its golf bag, "Vegetable matter deposited in swamps, naither you nor I ken the time ..."

"I ken it," I say." About 300 to 360 million years ago. My Carboniferous era."

"Then, those rotting plants," continues the bacteria, giving the ball a skillful tap, "consisting mostly of carbon, turn to sedimentary rock - coal - "

"And," concludes *Homo sapiens*, returning with arms full of flywheels, rocker arms, brass-silver boilers, safety valves, whistles, throttle valves, water level gauges, lube oil, and a bag of coal, "hundreds of millions of years later, revolutionize transportation, mining, agriculture, manufacturing - you name it - by providing fuel for the steam engine. And the labor and lives it's saved!" She starts clanking this piece of hardware onto that. Putting together something no doubt extremely brilliant.

"Weel," says the *P. azotogensis*, as the hare takes a hop toward its burrow, "I reckon we'll part away now. But if you're looking for mischief-makers, try Ireland. It's always been full of them."

"Not so fast," I say, shaking just enough to cause a handful of loose soil to drop into the entrance of the hare's burrow.

The hare freezes in its tracks, shaggy ears erect.

Sometimes you gotta get their attention.

"I'm hearing The Environment's hot and got a bullet with *Homo sapiens'* name, address and phone number on it. And a Fourier-philic dust mite (backed up by an extremely knowledgeable though unfortunately now departed yeast) says that your Mr. Watt is in all this like strep's in *Streptococcus*. Now what do you know? Spill!"

"A mite?" says the *P. Azotogensis*. "As in, a parasite?"

"Technically, dust mites are na parasites," explains an ear mite (*Psoroptes cuniculi*), looking up from its game of darts in the hare's ear, "since they only eat discarded dead tissue."

"Gross!" says the *P. azotogensis*.

"Och! And who is this fine gentleman that's grumphing at us then?" counters the ear mite. "Why, it's a bacteria! A dairty, disease-laden ..."

"I happen to be a *nitrogen-fixing* bacteria," the *P. azotogensis* interrupts.

"That's guid! That's wonderful! I'll ring you up if my nitrogen ever breaks."

"Na, na! I change nitrogen gas in the air into compounds which can be used by plants."

"I change nitrogen gas into compounds that can be used by plants," echoes the ear mite in a mocking sing-song. "Aye? Well, I bite rabbits' ears! So sue me!"

"All I'm saying is: Plants need me. The rabbit needs plants. You need the rabbit. So, basically, you depend on me," says the bacteria. "You're very welcome, by the way." And turning back to me: "Mr. Watt is a hero to all Scotland."

"To all *Homo sapiens* everywhere!" says *Homo sapiens*, wiping the grimy sweat off her forehead, as she dumps a bucket of water into the boiler.

"Do you see those?" the bacteria asks. It points with its long (9 micron), slender (.6 micron) flagellum to the horizon: Giant silver fans, each with three thin, pointed blades spinning slowly atop a silver pole as high as a forty-story building. Dozens and dozens of them.

"Wind turbines, 2.3 megawatts each," says the bacteria. "Mega *watts*. *Watts*. The basic unit of electricity, named after James Watt. Why? Because his invention made the generation of massive amounts of electricity practical. Ultimately, he ushered in the age of electricity. Modern life."

"Does your Monsieur le Dustmite prefer that we go back to horse-drawn plows and hand looms?" *Homo sapiens* demands, stepping back to admire her … I guess it's a steam engine … it looks like a cross between a huge unicycle and a small oil drill. She lights a fire in the coal bin under the boiler. You can hear the water building up a head of steam.

"All I know is it seemed pretty certain about this James Watt connection." I turn to the bacteria. "Now, I think you're holding out on me, and I think you better come clean, or ..."

Homo sapiens opens a valve. Steam rushes out of the boiler, pushing down the piston, which moves the flywheel. The cool, still air of the moor fills with smoke and chugging.

"They're very inventive," I explain to the bacteria and ear mite.

"Is that what ye call it?" says the bacteria, gathering up scattered golf clubs, the hare having dropped the bit of root when the chugging started.

"Inventive," the ear mite repeats, peeping out from under the hare's quivering, flattened ear, "Is that anything like desperately dementedly dangerous?"

"No worries," *Homo sapiens* shouts. "Earlier models were dangerous, but Watt gave this one all sorts of safety features. But to really accomplish something, we need more of them, and bigger ones." And she disappears again.

The ear mite, in an amazing acrobatic display, leaps from the hare's ear into mine and confides in a ticklish whisper, "Actually, Watt's invention may be very dangerous. Only you can't see the danger. Burning coal (and other carbon-based fossil fuels, like oil and natural gas) produces invisible gases that end up in your atmosphere and trap heat."

"Invisible gases, eh?"

"That's what they say," says the ear mite, and with another amazing jump, disappears back into the rabbit's ear.

"*They*. Ah yes, well *they* certainly couldn't be mistaken." On my knees now, I look the bacteria in the nucleoid. "I think you know more than you're saying! And don't give me invisible gas!"

"I dinna ken!" protests the bacteria. "Look, a couple of *Homo sapiens* were hiking up here the other day, and they were talking about The Environment and things getting warmer, and one of them said, 'Maybe it's the sun!'"

"Sol? Him and me been partners for 4,544,512,896 years, give or take. Turns out he's the source of just about 100 percent of my surface heat. Anyway, we've always had a good relationship."

"Naetheless," says the bacteria, "he is a thermonuclear reactor in your back yard, containing 99.86% of the mass of the entire solar system. You have to ask yourself if there are any safety issues there."

I've noticed Sol does vary some in the amount of heat he puts out. There are all kinds of cycles, ups and downs. Sometimes things can get a little bit screwy. Could that be what's got The Environment hot under the collar?

"I'm going to look into this," I warn the bacteria. "I'll get to the bottom of it. And if I find out you're trying to lay a bum rap on my partner ..."

"Niver!" says the bacteria. "I'm just saying, *maybe*. Who knows?"

"The sun may have some part in it, but I'd search oot those ghostly gases, as well," says the ear mite, just inches away, peeping out of the hare's ear. "Twa words: John Tyndall. Ireland."

I'm no mathematician, but if that's twa, our friend here is Bugs Bunny.

"And by the way," I ask the bacteria, "your Mr. Watt, I don't suppose he'd be … available for a little chat."

"Unpossible. He's ...."

"*Dead*???"

"Och, aye. He died in 1819."

"Of 'natural' causes, I suppose."

"It's likely. He was 83."

"What a coincidence. What a *strange* coincidence."

But if they're trying to scare me, well, okay, I'm trembling. I'm shaking like spacetime when two supermassive black holes merge. And I'm still not quitting.

The bacteria is trying to finger Sol. The mite says it's fossil fuels and invisible gases. It may be right. Invisible forces keep popping up in this investigation like dwarf planets in the Kuiper belt.

Just as the steam engine burns its last bit of coal and chugalunks to a halt, *Homo sapiens* comes back with more massive flywheels, immense rocker arms, gigantic boilers, enormous safety and throttle valves, huge whistles, humongous water level gauges, crates of lube oil, and colossal bags of coal.

I think I've learned everything I'm going to here. I gently pull *Homo sapiens* away from her no doubt brilliant but perhaps slightly unbalanced quest for power.

"Hey!" she protests. "Coal-fired electricity is key to our modern way of life!"

Her words seem to hang in the soft, hazy air for a moment, as the rain falls like a mild but chronic depressive tendency. The wind turbines whir in the distance; the wind whistles like endless loneliness through the stems of the heather. *What the heck is a Meltese Dodo?*

"C'mon, hon. Ireland. John Tyndall."

I take off my Glengarry cap and put on my flat Irish tweed.

VI.

"Oh, aye, John Tyndall!" it says in its flat Belfast accent. "A brilliant *Homo sapiens*! He wrote about my anti-bacterial properties fifty years before Alexander Fleming, who won the Nobel Prize for it. But then, since ancient times, the wise women had treated infected wounds with blue moldy bread. It just took the brainiacs a wee bit to catch up."

It's hard to spend three minutes with a blue mold without Penicillin popping up in the conversation. Not that you can blame them.

"Sounds like a smart guy," I say. "Ever notice that smart guys cause most of the trouble in this world? So perhaps you could enlighten me: Supposing a party (or parties) unknown was making things hot for The Environment, which (with motives as yet undetermined, but perhaps relating to a Meltese Dodo) was suspected of gunning for *Homo sapiens*. How would you see John Tyndall fitting into that picture?"

"His work," says the mold, "is so broad and far-reaching - it's at the foundation of a small handful of ologies, ometries and oscopies - he could probably fit into almost any picture. I'm told they are very proud of him down in Leighlinbridge. I imagine they can tell yez everything ye need to know."

It gives me directions to County Carlow, and I thank it for its time.

"No trouble at all." It turns to *Homo sapiens*. "And should you ever suffer a wound which becomes inflamed or abscessed ..."

"I won't hesitate to call."

"Even a pustule."

"Thank you so much."

"A pimple."

"You're too kind ..."

"A furuncle, a carbuncle ..."

Its voice fades as we head south.

* * *

"So, you've heard of John Tyndall?" I ask the Desmoulin's Whorl Snail (*Vertigo moulinsiana*), relaxing with a pint (for a snail) of river water and a mouthful (for a snail) of microfungi on some decaying vegetation in a bed of reeds by the River Barrow.

"The famous scientist? Sure, who hasn't?" says the snail. "Sit down. Care for a pint?"

"Don't mind if I ..."

"Hey!" says *Homo sapiens*, leaning in close to the reed. "You're a snail! I had you in France! You're great with garlic and butter!"

The snail pulls into its shell, its tiny eyestalks bugging out and vibrating like clangers on a doorbell.

"Is that *Homo sapiens*!?" the snail whispers to me. "They're omnivorous, you know. Is it following you?"

"No! Well ... maybe."

"What does it want?" the snail asks in a hoarse whisper.

"I don't know, exactly. See, it hired me, and followed me to France ..."

"France! France!" the snail's terrified squeak echoes up from deep within its protective shell.

"Easy, easy," I pat what I can only assume is the shoulder of the snail's shell comfortingly. Then to *Homo sapiens*: "I think you got our friend a little spooked, hon. Maybe you could … take a walk?"

Homo sapiens shrugs and takes off.

"With *Homo sapiens*," says the snail, "if you're not furry and cute, you're nothing at all."

It serves me a tiny pint and takes a sip from its own. We raise our glasses in a silent toast.

"Yeah, I guess. Still, she's kinda cute, ain't she?" I say, watching her wander upstream. "But, look, I'm on this case, and ..."

"Does it have anything to do with *Homo sapiens*?"

"Well, yeah …"

"I don't want to get involved."

"I mean, probably. Maybe."

"No offense. But I'm really glad you asked it to move along."

"Look, maybe it has nothing to do with *Homo sapiens*. In fact, did you happen to notice anything unusual about the sun?"

"I've noticed that it shines on the good and evil alike. That seems a bit odd to me."

"Hmm. Could that affect The Environment?"

"Don't see how."

"Look, uh, I gotta ask you about something. Got to follow up every lead, no matter how silly it seems. You wouldn't know anything about - ha ha! - invisible gases?"

The snail chews its microfungi thoughtfully for a moment.

"Tyndall spent a lot of time in the Swiss Alps, mountain climbing and studying how glaciers grow."

"That's great! Wonderful! Mountain climbing. How enjoyable. Now …"

"He became convinced that Europe must have once been covered with ice. Which was controversial back then. A lot of scientists thought that you had just been getting steadily colder since you'd been born. The idea of a past ice age with subsequent warming didn't fit their preconceptions."

"Scientists! Who can figure them? But look, I'm working a case, and I've got these leads I need to follow up on ..."

"Tyndall wanted to come up with a logical explanation for your alternating hot and cold periods. He thought changes in your atmosphere could have something to do with it, based on Fourier's idea that your atmosphere keeps you warm. So Tyndall did experiments to determine which gases in your atmosphere would trap radiant heat and re-radiate some of it back towards your surface."

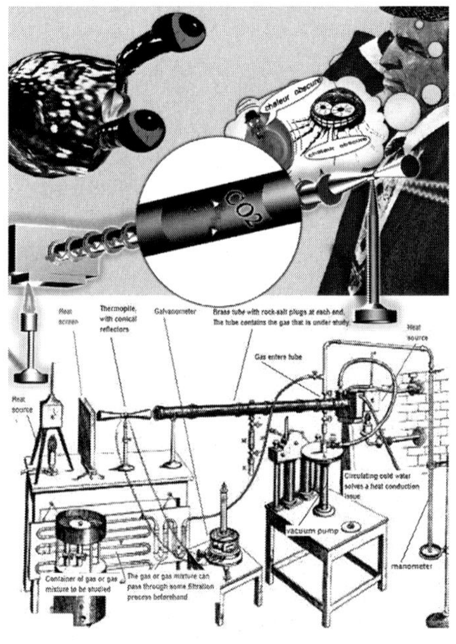

"Radiant heat, like sunlight?"

"Not exactly. Tyndall was interested in the heat that's radiated back from your surface out into your atmosphere after sunlight hits and warms you. That radiant heat is invisible; it's all below red on the spectrum."

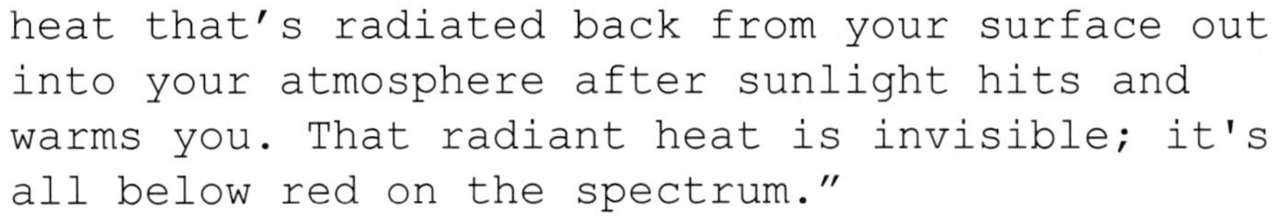

"Like Herschel's thermometer just below the red end of the spectrum, which registered a higher temperature than either of the others!"

"William Herschel. Aye. Although what that thermometer showed was infrared energy coming directly from the sun - which is just forty-nine percent of the sun's energy, the rest being mostly visible light. Fourier and Tyndall were interested in the infrared energy *you* emit, after *all* of the sun's energy - ultraviolet, visible and infrared - hits you and is transformed into infrared radiant heat. Because it was invisible, Tyndall called that energy 'obscure radiation' or 'dark waves'."

Chaleur obscure echoes in my head. First in the pipsy squeak of a Fourier-frenzied French dust mite. Then in the light-hearted lilt of a doomed *Saccharomyces cerevisiae* in Slough.

"Today, we refer to it as 'infrared light', 'radiant heat' or simply 'heat'," continues the snail. "Though not all radiant heat is infrared. Something that's red hot or white hot is radiating heat in the visible spectrum. In any case, Tyndall built an apparatus with a tube he could fill with any gas, such as hydrogen, oxygen, nitrogen, carbon dioxide, or air. He'd fill the tube with a particular gas. Then he'd radiate heat into the tube at one end and see how much heat came out the other end. Care for another drink?"

"Thank you."

"He found that carbon dioxide blocked radiant heat. But oxygen, hydrogen and nitrogen didn't. Also, that moist air absorbed a lot of the heat, while dry air absorbed much less. Tyndall concluded that 'the vapor screen' of your atmosphere keeps you warm because it offers almost no hindrance to the inflow of visible light from the sun but significantly blocks the outflow of heat into space."

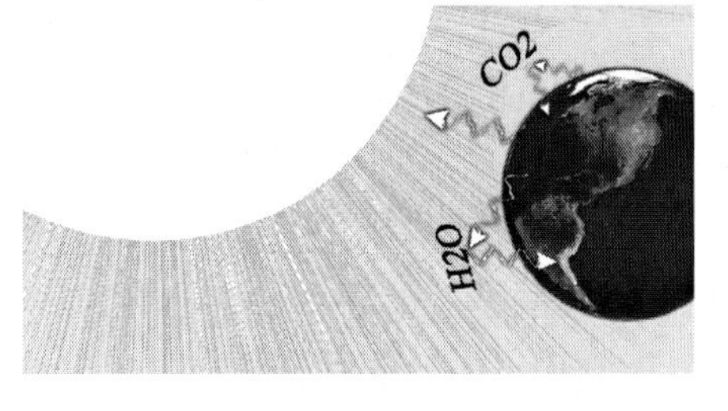

The same thing Fourier said!

"Amazing, isn't it?" says the snail. "Water vapor: invisible, seemingly insubstantial. And yet without it, you - no disrespect intended - would be nothing but a big ball of ice."

"You know, one thing I don't get is, if energy is coming in and can't get back out, why don't I just keep getting hotter and hotter forever?"

"Because," says the snail, "the warmer you get, the more energy you radiate back into space. Think of a piece of metal. Heat it a little, it gets red hot. Heat it more, it gets white hot. When it's white hot, it's radiating a lot more heat than when it's just red hot. Your heat is invisible, so you can't see the change. But still, you radiate more as you heat up. Eventually, you reach an equilibrium point, where incoming and outgoing energy are equal. At that point, you stop warming. But the more your atmosphere insulates you, the warmer you have to get to reach that point of equilibrium." The snail yawns. "Well, it's getting to be my bedtime."

"Hold on. I don't suppose there'd be any objection to me speaking with Mr. Tyndall, just to verify what you've told me?"

"I'm sorry, but he's ..."

"Don't tell me: *Dead*."

"Aye. In 1893."

"No suspicious circumstances surrounding his passing, I don't suppose? Nothing to do with a Meltese Dodo?"

"He was accidentally poisoned by his wife."

"Oh, well, nothing unusual there. Accidents happen every day."

The snail curls into its shell, with a tiny, bubbly snore.

The River Barrow reflects flat gray clouds, rippling past the broken mirror image of a gently rocking blue rowboat, gliding down to the chocolate shadow of a ruined black stone castle standing sentinel over an ancient stone bridge of nine arches.

No leads. No viable suspects. I got nothing. Nothing but a case with more black holes in it than the observable universe.

Time to wake someone up.

"You ever heard of The Extinctor?"

The snail wakes up - quick (relative to other things it's done so far).

"Know him?" I ask.

"Know him?" says the snail, "I get threatening notes from him every year."

"Yeah? Well, he's a pal of mine. Maybe I could put in a good word for you. But you got to tell me everything you know."

"I already told you everything," says the snail.

Dark heat. Invisible light. Water vapor. Carbon dioxide. Fourier. Herschel. Watt. Tyndall. There's some kind of pattern here, but I just can't put it together. Like trying to read a map through a kaleidoscope.

"The smallest fact," I say, "something that may seem totally insignificant to you, could be the key."

"Well," says the snail, "I once overheard two fishermen talking about The Environment, and global warming. They blamed it all on … what was it they said? It was two words ..."

"It would be."

Homo sapiens shows up, with a sharpened stick raised above her head, following a thin, exhausted, pale, reddish salmon.

"Something tells me she's about to be omnivorous," the snail frets.

"The two words," I remind the snail.

"You'll talk to The Extinctor?"

"Promise."

"Put in a good word for my mate, the salmon, as well?"

"Yes, yes. Promise."

"Internal Combustion!"

Which has a certain credibility, if only because it actually is two words.

"Internal Combustion. So who is this guy? *Where* is he?"

"I don't know," says the snail. "The fishermen mentioned America. And Big Oil."

"America. Thanks." I run after *Homo sapiens*.

"Best of luck to you," the snail calls out.

"Wait a minute!" I call back to the snail. "Do you happen to know any American bacteria?"

The snail shakes its head. The salmon just keeps on swimming away, with *Homo sapiens* right behind it.

"Or molds? Yeasts?"

The next sound out of the snail is a tiny, bubbly snore.

"Even a mildew would be helpful," I call out, still following the salmon and *Homo sapiens* downstream.

"Sorry, us salmon, we try to avoid bacteria, fungi and things like that; they're not good for us," says the salmon.

"I need a source with local knowledge in America. You know, on the down and dirty."

"Down and dirty?" says the salmon. "You might try the Cuyahoga River, in Ohio."

VII.

We don't have to do too much sole-searching before I'm tipping my fedora to the Cuyahoga.

Homo sapiens looks around appreciatively at the trees and flowers bowing slowly in the breeze like a brigade of totally beyond-it Buddhist monks. She breathes in the fresh air and sighs like a guy who just won the last throw in a craps game, putting him square for the night. And she begins lovingly building something which could possibly be a nature center.

"Is it building a nature observatory and nature center for nature talks and natural history lectures?" gurgles the stream, as it twists and turns along its course.

"Yeah. Yeah. Sure. Now, about this Internal Combustion ..."

"Well, I know what *combustion* is," burbles the stream. "That's when they dam you up and dredge you out so you don't flow very well, and then dump you full of oil, gasoline, dyes, acids, trash, and sewage, and then something - like a spark from a railroad track or some red-hot molten steel they dump into you - lights you on fire. And then maybe you light boats or office buildings - or whatever else happens to be around - on fire. That happened to me in 1868 ... and 1883 ...and 1887 and 1912 and 1922 and 1936 and 1941 and 1948 and 1952 and 1969.

"Luckily, there were a lot of reporters around for the last one, because Cleveland (which is where I empty into Lake Erie) had just elected the first black mayor in America. So the 1969 fire - even though it was minor by comparison with the one in 1952 - became big news and triggered a lot of reforms in the early 1970's, including the Clean Water Act and the formation of the Environmental Protection Agency.

"Today, things are much better. You might say I *sparked* the environmental movement," the river concludes proudly, with a twinkle in its water. "In my National Park, I now have beaver, otter, mink, muskrat, raccoon, coyote, deer. I've got a bald eagle nesting at Pinery Narrows!"

"The algae might know," says a fish foraging along the bottom of the river, gobbling up drowned insects with big protruding lips.

"He's a Hog Snorter," says the Cuyahoga, with evident pride. "They're moderately sensitive to pollution, yet they're one of my most common fish now."

"Hog *Sucker*," says the fish, "Northern Hog Sucker. Sheesh. It's bad enough without you making it worse."

"The point is, how *clean* I am," says the Cuyahoga. "Did you know that the beaver reclaimed what used to be an automobile junk yard, turned it into a wetland, and now I've got herons, turtles, frogs ..."

"But the planet is asking about *internal combustion*, not how clean you are. And just the other day I was passing a little pool near a dam, and I overheard some blue-green algae saying how, without them, internal combustion would never have succeeded."

"Blue-green algae. You mean like that mob of cyanobacteria hanging out in Lake Erie?" says the Cuyahoga, a shivering ripple passing over its surface.

"The same," says the Hog Sucker.

"I hear they're pure poison."

"Don't you have a mouth on you!" says a blue-green algae floating by. "We're just trying to make a living, like everybody else."

"I wouldn't know personally," the river rushes to explain, "The edge of the lake is as far as I go."

"My name's Cy," the algae says to me. "Come on, I'll introduce you around. And don't worry about what the river said; we're not that toxic - under most conditions."

I hear a banging sound, turn around and find *Homo sapiens* hammering up a billboard-size sign: "Grand Opening: Coal-Fired Nuclear Power Plant and Pesticide-Insecticide-Fungicide-Herbicide-Atomic-Bomb Factory".

I take the sign down. Tear down the power plant and the factory. Replant greenery. Take *Homo sapiens* gently by the hand, and lead her away with me.

A light but steady rain begins to fall.

* * *

Cy leads us to the western end of Lake Erie, dominated by the *Microcystis aeruginosa*, mobbed up in a glistening bluish-green scum.

I note with relief that *Homo sapiens* has wandered off to a stretch of rocky, sparsely vegetated soil that presents no very obvious or attractive opportunities for killing anything. In fact, believe it or not, she actually seems to be promoting life: lovingly tilling a patch of soil, scattering grass seed, spreading fertilizer.

Cy points to the *M. aeruginosa*, thick as pea soup, slick as paint. "That scum over there - that's The Blue-Green Mob, headed up Mike Rocystin. Looks like we could be a bit deadly today. Lot of phosphorus coming into the neighborhood, brings out the worst in us. And there's Al G and the West End Gang. Came out of nowhere and just took over."

When we get to the water's edge, Cy introduces me to his pals: "This is our friend, the planet. He's all right."

"*Slurp, slurp, slurpslurpslurp.*" His buddies seem to really be enjoying the run-off coming into the lake.

"We love that phosphorus!" Cy explains.

Then Cy tells its friends that I've got a few questions for them.

"Nothing personal, I hope," says Mike. "Snoops come poking around here asking personal questions ... *slurp* … it could be bad for their health."

"No, no. It's just I heard good things about you. Got a little curious. Word in the watershed is that without you, Internal Combustion would of flopped like coho salmon in a warm, shallow pond."

Mike grins. "It would of ... *slurp* … gone south like a Cleveland godfather indicted for tax evasion."

"It would of folded up like a ... *slurp* … AK-47 in a violin case," says Al.

"It woulda disappeared like Joey Juice after he ratted out ... *slurp* … Allie G.," says Mike.

"Now, I don't suppose," I say, "that you might have heard anything about where Internal Combustion might be, or might have been at such time as any heat might theoretically have been applied to The Environment?"

"The Environment? *Slurp!* The psycho mass serial killer?" asks Mike. "I'd love to meet the guy. I've always admired his work."

"I'll introduce you. Anyway, like I say, it looks like somebody's putting heat on the guy, possibly using invisible gases, and The Environment's not taking it too kindly."

While keeping one eye on *Homo sapiens* - who is pacing her lawn with her fertilizer spreader like a lioness in a cage - I give them the lowdown on the case.

"We don't know nothing about that, do we Al? *Slurrrp!*"

"Nothing whatsoever. *Slurrrrp!*"

"Or a Meltese Dodo?"

"Now, that just sounds dumb," says Mike. "In fact, I gotta tell you, I'm not buying this whole story. I mean, The Environment's a big operator - they say he's got a hand in everything. How could you threaten a big shot like that? *Watch out, or I'll hit you with my invisible gases!!!???"*

Mike, Al and their buddies have a good chortle. I'm not getting anywhere here. I guess it's true what they say: A kind word and a friendly smile never get you as far as a kind word, a friendly smile, and a credible threat.

"That's too bad," I say, softly. "Because I would hate to have to go to the University of Toledo's Lake Erie Center and get a lake scientist to come down here with a graduate student and take some, uh, *samples*. Maybe bring some of you fine, upstanding lake scum into the lab and test you for … *toxins*?"

"Speaking strictly theoretically," says Mike, suddenly imbued with a new spirit of cooperation, "I would speculate that in Mr. Watt's steam engine - based on combustion of the *external* variety - coal would be burned to create steam; and that steam would move a piston in a cylinder. In short, combustion would occur *outside* the cylinder.

"While, in contrast, with *internal* combustion, I would imagine that fuel would explode *inside* the cylinder, producing high pressure gases, which would directly move the piston in the cylinder."

"Very interesting. And where would I find this cylinder?"

"In almost any car, airplane or boat," says Al.

"But one thing is required," says Mike, "namely, a high-density fuel such as gasoline. *Slurp!* Without that, the force of the explosion would be insufficient for the purpose, reminding one of Jimmy Valentine's lament after his eighth failed attempt to ice Frankie M.

" 'Roses ain't blue,
Violets ain't red,
I blew up your Lincoln,
So why ain't you dead?'

"And that," says Mike, "is where we come in: Gasoline comes from oil. And oil comes from us - algae."

"Correct," says Al. "At various times, large numbers of tiny sea plants - mostly algae - and sea creatures died and got buried on the ocean floor."

"Yeah, I remember," I say. "Late Jurassic. Cretaceous. Never pinned that on anyone."

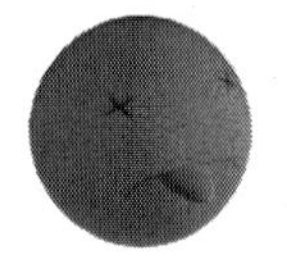

"These dead individuals ..." says Al.

"Who - I would speculate - got what was coming to them," says Mike.

"... got covered by tons and tons of silt and sand and mud … *slurp* … creating intense pressure and heat ..."

"Possibly they failed to show proper respect."

"... which, over millions of years, converted them into oil and gas."

Fossil fuels. Which the ear mite said produce invisible gases.

"Bacteria finally broke 'em down," says Mike.

"Even algae can take only so much."

"So this heat that someone's applying to The Environment ..."

"We don't know nothing about this," says Al, sinking below the water, which is thick with the green mob.

"Word on the water," I say "is that Internal Combustion's greasy prints are all over the job. Now, if The Environment hears that *you* aided and abetted Internal Combustion ..."

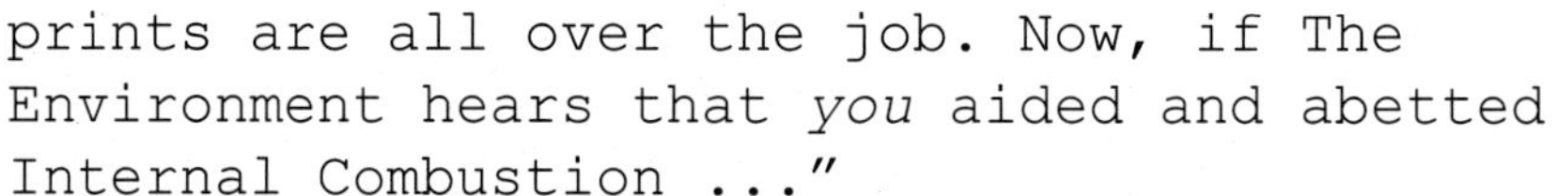

"We had nothing to do with it. We was at the dogfish track at the time." Al seems barely able to get out the next sentence. "Which we have - a thousand witnesses who will testify."

"Yeah. I bet. All of 'em blue-green."

"We was - " Mike is also sinking, weak, gasping, "nowhere - near - that job."

"What's wrong?" I ask. "What's happening?"

"Algae on top - keep sunlight - from reaching - ones below. Can't live - without sunlight for photosynthesis. We're - going down."

"Scum on top - keeps oxygen in atmosphere - from mixing - into water. Perhaps like this - when algae died - millions of years ago - formed oil."

"You're dying. You got nothing to hide now, nothing to lose. Help me out: What does Internal Combustion have to do with The Environment?"

"Burning gasoline," Mike coughs, "produces carbon dioxide - CO2."

"Svante Arrhenius," Al gasps.

And they're gone.

I look around and realize that millions of the algae are dying, murdered by their own mob. A gang war!

"Hey, doll, we better scram."

As we walk, I try to explain why it's just not working out to have her hanging around all the time.

"Blue-green algae seem nice enough on surface," says a zebra mussel, in a thick Russian accent, "but underneath … ptooey!" It spits out blue-green algae even as it chomps up other microscopic life forms.

"I don't remember seeing you around here before," I say.

"We are here long time. Introduced by foreign ships emptying ballast. Before, conditions not right for us to multiply. Water warmer now. Heh heh!"

"Did you hear what Al said just before he died: something like 'Sfahntuh Arayneeyoose'?" I ask the mussel.

"*Da*. Svante Arrhenius," the zebra mussel says. "Swedish scientist."

"Thanks. I'll follow up on that."

"Say *privyet* to cousins over there, colonizing Lake Mälaren."

"Will do! And maybe they can help me out. Always great to have a local source. You know, on the down and dirty."

"*Da*. Down, dirty. Zebra mussels usually live at moderate depth and accumulate organic pollutants like PCBs by filtering water."

"So you're actually cleaning up the water?" *Homo sapiens* asks.

"*Da*. Since we came from *Rossiya*, water got a lot clearer here."

"The extra sunlight in my water," says Lake Erie, "probably encouraged these huge toxic algae blooms. The zebra mussels also starve fish by eating microorganisms. They clog water intake pipes and hurt native clams by attaching to them. Plus, the pollutants they accumulate get passed on to fish and birds that eat them, and then to other life forms that eat the fish and birds. Tell Lake Mälaren to watch out!"

"Hey, look over there!" I point and shout.

When *Homo sapiens* looks the other way, I take off for Sweden.

VIII.

I pull up the ear flaps and loosen the chin strap on my brown fur hat. Pearly ocean reflects pearl gray sky.

"A-a-a-aye a-a-aye a-a-a-a-aye." The wandering band of tiny warm-water zooplankton (*Calanus helgolandicus*) beats out an insistent, syncopated rhythm with their mouth appendages. Their lean, low biomass bodies flash silver in the sunlight as they dance through the North Atlantic.

A raw, passionate voice rises through the tossing waves: "Corriente de océano-oo-o-o, por que estoy aqui, yo-o-oo-o?" The others echo: "Por que estoy aqui, yo-o-oo-o?"

Ocean current, why am I here? Why am I here?

"Aquí tu calor me trajo-o-oo-o."

Your heat brought me here.

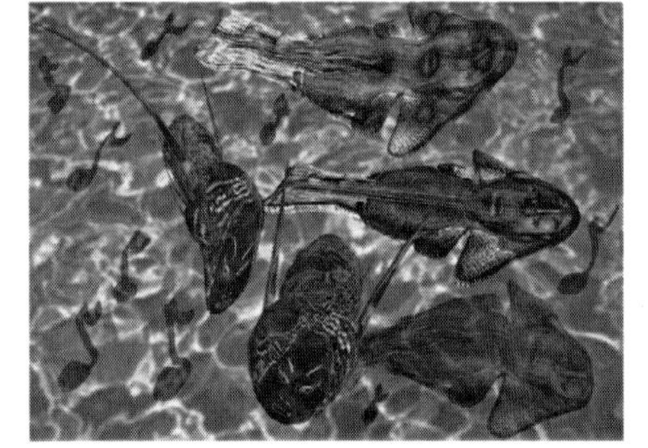

The wild, weeping strains of a fiddle fish (*Squatina squatina*) mingle with the throaty, throbbing lamentation of the singers.

When they fall silent for a moment, I say, "Excuse me, I'm looking for Svante Arrhenius - the Swedish scientist? And the Meltese Dodo. It's very important."

"Very sorry, señor, we are new here. Perhaps you can find one of the natives, *Calanus finmarchicus*. *Lamentablemente*, most them have moved north, and besides, there are not many of them at this time of the year."

The skeleton of a baby codfish floats by.

"Ay! Poor little fellows," comments the *C. helgolandicus.* "They used to eat *C. finmarchicus.* Now they have only us. We, *desafortunadamente*, are lean and come at the wrong time of year. So they starve."

"I am so sorry. But I really gotta find Svante Arrhenius. Maybe you know where Lake Mälaren is?"

"*Pues*, Sweden is that way ..." it says, pointing eastward.

* * *

Lake Mälaren just shimmers quietly in the distance, saying nothing, as we bob gently up and down in the little open boat.

"I don't think lakes talk much," says the tiny, walnut-shaped American comb jelly (*Mnemiopsis leidyi)*, shimmering as its tiny hairs beat the water to propel it forward through the briny green of the Baltic Sea in search of fish eggs, fish larvae, and zooplankton.

"The one in America did," says *Homo sapiens* brightly, as she tests the balance of her fishing pole and skewers a live herring on a hook. (Yeah, she showed up just as I was getting into the boat. I tried to talk to her, but if you think she listened, I've got some beach-front property on Venus I'd like to sell you.)

"Well, here in Sweden, they tend to be a bit more reserved," says the American comb jelly. "If you're looking for conversation, try the foreigners, like me. I'm friendly and outgoing, if sometimes slightly naïve and childish. Or the fishhook water flea. It's talkative and extroverted, though somewhat aggressive, abrasive, loud and opinionated."

A nearby fishhook water flea (*Cercopagis pengoi*) sucks the juices out of an even tinier floating crustacean, captured using the flea's two long front legs and now held between three shorter pairs of legs. "*Yum! Yum!* That's a filthy, foul, dirty, sea-licey lie! We're not really extroverted. We just act extroverted to cover up our natural shyness!"

Homo sapiens' fishing line arches elegantly into the water and, suddenly taut, strains back towards the boat. Apparently, she's having some luck. Good for her. Me, I don't have time for fishing. I have other things to worry about.

"So, you know more than you're letting on?" I say to Lake Mälaren. "Why so reserved? Got something to hide? Like maybe a little *Internal Combustion*? Well, I got it from a highly dependable Great Lake in North America that your Mr. Arrhenius is mixed up in this thing like bacteria in soil. Now, if you take my advice ..."

"You're the one that's mixed up!" says the fishhook water flea, its voice a sharp, scolding little screech. "Svante Arrhenius was the first to calculate mathematically how much you would warm up as a result of a given concentration of carbon dioxide in your atmosphere!"

"Yeah!" affirms a chorus of thousands - no millions - of nearby fishhook water fleas.

"Warm up! Aha!" I say. "And he was the first to calculate it? Now isn't that interesting? A mere curious coincidence, no doubt. Unless he's actually *behind the whole thing*!"

"I suppose it helped," says the water flea, its sarcastic little screech cutting through the brackish water like a new razor, "that he was a Nobel-Prize-winning physicist and chemist. And that he had studied the work of many great scientists who had come before him, including Tyndall and Fourier. Even with all his genius, it took Arrhenius a year, working 14 hour days, to make the calculations."

"That's right!" shouts the fishhook water flea chorus.

Homo sapiens' fishing line comes up covered with what looks like wads of wet cotton. When she tries to reel it in, as the line goes through the little metal ring on the tip of the pole, the cottony stuff sticks and catches, and before you know it, the ring is as full of it as a congressman addressing a church group, and *Homo sapiens* can't reel in anymore. After jerking her pole up, down, sideways and around, letting the line out and trying to reel it back half a dozen times, she cuts the line and tosses the pole to the floor of the boat, at the same asking loudly - not in exactly these words, yet in language highly appropriate to her new sailing profession - what this unfortunate cottony substance might be.

"It's us!" the water flea answers, loud and proud. "Thousands of us. No, millions of us. We stick together. We may be small ..."

"But you got a big mouth. Now look, this Arrhenius guy. Sounds like he really wanted to know all about how this warming worked. Perhaps because he was … *planning something*?"

"Or perhaps because you are definitely an idiot. His marriage had just fallen apart. He was depressed and needed something to throw himself into. So he divided your whole surface into small squares ..."

"Funny, I don't remember that. Sounds like it would hurt."

Homo sapiens picks up a large folded fishing net from the floor of the boat and casts it in a curvaceous arch into the water.

"He did it in an Atlas, genius." At which the flea chorus forms itself into the shape of a book.

"Oh."

"For each square ..."

The book opens. The pages are divided into a grid of tiny squares, some brighter and some darker, which the fishhook water flea taps, using its hooked tail as a pointer.

"... he came up with an estimate for albedo."

"So, he was partnered up with this Al what's-his-name?" I ask.

Homo sapiens is trying to pull her net back in, but it's clogged and heavy with jelly-like, gluey masses of fishhook water fleas, singing "The more we stick together, together, together ..." Trying to pull the net back into the boat, she struggles, slips, slides, and - trying to keep herself in the boat - grabs onto me, and plop! we both go into the drink.

"Albedo is reflectivity," says the water flea, more quietly now that we're basically face to face, "from bright white ice *reflecting* 80% or more of solar radiation, to dark ocean *absorbing* 80% or more." The fishhook water fleas act out this ancient dance of sun, land and light, in something that could perhaps be compared to tableau vivant, water polo, acrobatic surfing, ballet, mime, and a million car pile-up at rush-hour. "This number would tell him how much solar energy would get absorbed and turn into infrared versus how much would just get reflected and bounce back into space as visible light."

Fourier's idea again, I muse.

Homo sapiens tries to climb back on the boat using me as a gangplank. We both end up way over our heads in cold, salty water.

"Of course, albedo would change with the seasons," says the water flea (who, naturally, is quite comfortable conversing underwater), "because of changing snow cover, freezing and melting of the Arctic Ocean, changing vegetation, and so on. He took all that into account. He also took into account the fact that, over time, as you warmed, more snow and ice would melt, and your surface would get darker and less reflective."

"Hmm," I say, as I surface, covered with a heavy, sticky blanket of fishhook water fleas. "Which would make me still warmer. Which would melt more snow and ice ..."

"Bingo! A positive feedback loop. And increasing warmth could also create more water vapor, a greenhouse gas which would warm you even more - another positive feedback loop."

Homo sapiens comes up, grabs the side of the boat. She pulls, grapples, grasps, grunts, groans, but she's covered with fishhook water fleas like me, and she just can't make it.

"It seems like it would never end," I say. "You know, I wonder if that's what happened to Venus back in the day. I remember when the Venusian oceans boiled away. Kinda shook me up. Made me wonder if the same thing might happen to me. Is that what Arrhenius predicted?"

"Venus is a 'runaway greenhouse' planet. Arrhenius didn't project anything like that for you. When he calculated how different concentrations of CO2 (which he called 'carbonic acid') would affect temperatures at different latitudes in different seasons, taking into account all the feedback loops (like water vapor and albedo) that amplify the effect of the CO2, he calculated that you would warm 4° - 5° Celsius (6° - 9° Fahrenheit) if the carbon dioxide in your atmosphere doubled."

"That's a lot of hot."

"Which I would probably appreciate, for example, since I tend to like warmer waters. But it's not a sixteenth of what it would take to make your oceans boil."

"Whew! But … how do we know Arrhenius was right?"

"Well, a lot of his predictions have come true. For example, in the article he published, 'On the Influence of Carbonic Acid in the Air upon the Temperature of the Ground', Arrhenius said that warming would increase as you go from the equator to the poles, that nights would warm more than days, winter more than summer, and land more than sea. Every one of these predictions has now been confirmed by observation and by computer models."

No way that's a coincidence.

"And where was our clever Mr. Arrhenius when all this warming took place? Does he have an alibi?"

"I'd say so: He's been dead for over 75 years."

"Dead!"

"Yes. He published his paper in 1896 and died in 1927."

So much death. Like stumbling into a cluster of red super giants during a Hydrogen drought.

"By the way," I call over to Lake Mälaren, "if you've got any zebra mussels ..."

"Yah, I've got them."

"Well, tell them their cousins in Lake Erie say hi."

"Lake Erie!" says the fishhook water flea, "Is it as glorious as they say? Warm, shallow water! Rich in nutrients! I think I'll go find a boat headed over that way and see if I can catch a ride in their ballast water."

"Wait! How did Arrhenius die? Were there any Meltese Dodos in the vicinity? Did he have any enemies?"

"Well, he was generally a congenial, happy man, dedicated to science and helping the world, so I'm sure everyone hated him. Now, if you'll excuse me ..."

Hmph! Smart mouth little nipper. But, still, how true it is that the that the "perfect" life is often the perfect cover for the perfect crime.

"One more thing! Had he argued with anybody recently?"

"Well ... There was Knut Ångström."

"Aha! Did you know that, when stressed, some newts sweat that most lethal of neurotoxins: tetrodotoxin?"

"Not newt, Sherlock! *Ka-noot*! With a *K*."

"Don't get your axis in a tilt," I say calmly. "Where was this *Ka-noot* at the time of the murder?"

"Murder? There was a scientific disagreement. Arrhenius calculated that you would warm 4° - 5° Celsius (6° - 9° Fahrenheit) if the carbon dioxide in your atmosphere doubled. Knut criticized Arrhenius. Said it wouldn't warm that much."

"Aha! So perhaps Knut, fearing that Arrhenius will spread panic with his false and exaggerated claims, prepares a fatal dose of tetrodotoxin and ..."

"Current estimates are 2 - 4.5 ° Celsius, so Arrhenius was actually amazingly accurate. And the measure he developed - what will happen to temperature if carbon dioxide doubles over preindustrial levels - has become a standard metric in climate science known as 'climate sensitivity'."

"So both Arrhenius and Knut knew that increasing concentrations of carbon dioxide would affect The Environment? And yet, rather than alert the authorities, they sit around arguing about exactly how many degrees …"

"Fiddle fish sticks! Like most scientists of his time, Arrhenius was more curious about the cause of past cooling - specifically the ice ages - than worried about the consequences of any future warming. Anyway, he thought the doubling of CO2 would take 3000 years - which was probably fair, at the rate fossil fuels were being used in the late 1890's. (Of course, after that, the rate increased exponentially.)

"He also assumed warming would bring *good* things: milder climates, longer growing seasons. In fact, back then, pretty much everyone who thought about these things at all - like Guy Callendar, for instance, the British steam engineer and inventor who picked up the ball from Arrhenius - thought that."

"What was that name? Guy ..."

"C-a-l-l-e-n-d-a-r. A British engineer."

"And, to be fair," a silver birch (*Betula pendula*) calls out, its clear, high, resonant voice ringing like chimes from a distant hilltop, "climate change actually *is* bringing longer growing seasons and increased harvests to Sweden, and maybe even new crops. It's also bringing more pests, weeds, droughts and floods. But if you just look at agriculture in Sweden, the overall effect is positive for now.

"Also, if warming had been slower, it would have been more benign. In fact, one could imagine a scenario in which extremely moderate and controlled burning of fossil fuels could warm you *just slowly and gently enough* to compensate for the effects of the Milankovitch cycles, and thus avert the next ice age without causing any other problems."

"Milan … ?"

"Milutin M-i-l-a-n-k-o-v-i-t-c-h. The Serbian engineer and geophysicist who calculated how your relationship to the sun - the shape of your orbit, the tilt of your axis - basically determines your climate on a scale of tens of thousands to hundreds of thousands of years," says the silver birch.

"Determines my climate! That could be the answer to the whole mystery! Well, I've been meaning to have a talk with Sol anyway."

IX.

Dripping wet, but drying rapidly as steam rises from my clothes, I take off my hat and shield my eyes as I get used to Sol's glare.

"Hey, Sol!" I call out. "Sorry to bother you ...".

"No problem," he says in that effusive, explosive way of his. "Good to hear from you once in a while. How you doing?"

"All right, I guess. Got a little fever," I admit.

"Fever! Ha! You ain't seen fever, kid, till you've fused hydrogen into helium. Try 383 yottawatts!"

"Wow. That's a yottawatts."

"Ha ha ha! Hey, here's one: This carbo-dioxo-cephalic bottom-feeding Venusian bog beast walks in and sits down at the bar. So the bartender says, 'Hey, why the long face?' Ha ha ha ha!"

"Ha ha! So, you're feeling good?" I ask Sol.

"Not too bad. I'm in kind of a low right now, actually."

"Really."

"No big thing. Just the usual eleven-year cycle. It averages out. The low just happens to be a little more extended this time. When you start seeing increasing sunspots, you'll know I'm on my way up again, and you'll be getting a little more irradiance."

"Reason I ask, I was just talking to this silver birch, real nice gal, and she reminded me that my relationship with you - the shape of my orbit, the tilt of my axis - basically determines my climate. Apparently this guy Milankovitch has got this all figured out."

"Oh, yeah. Milankovitch cycles: stretch, wobble and tilt."

"Please! Eccentricity, precession and obliquity!" says Mercury, who has a bad habit of listening in to other celestial bodies' conversations.

"Like I said: stretch, wobble and tilt," says Sol, grinning.

"Now, Sol," I say, "you and me go way back, and you've always been a good pal." I take a deep breath. "But I'm working a case where your name has come up several times. And, you understand, I gotta look at all the angles."

"What kind of case?"

So, I run it down for him. *Homo sapiens*. The Environment. The heat. The Meltese Dodo. The leads. The mysterious deaths.

"I'd watch out, if I were you," says Venus, who happens to be orbiting slinkily nearby. "It sounds to me like you may be heading for a tipping point."

What a voice! Pure velvet. Even when she's warning you of impending doom, you'd think she was asking if you'd like powdered galactose on your raspberry nebula cream cupcakes.

"Perhaps we could go out to dinner and you could tell me exactly what you think I should watch out for?" I suggest. "And if I tip over, you could catch me."

"I'm not kidding," says Venus. "Do you know what a tipping point is?"

"Is that after you finish your meal at the Deepspace Diner, when you give the waitron extra money if you haven't contracted entero-pathogenic pantophagous planetary food poisoning?"

"No. It's more like the two Alpha Centaurian abstract transcendental mathematicians who are on vacation, and their cruise saucer stops at Earth for the day. They decide they want to experience the primitive forms of transportation used there. So they buy tickets on a four-engine jet flying from Los Angeles to New York. And they're discussing how amazing it is that it will take more than five hours to go less than 1.28-10 parsecs, when the captain announces that one of the engines has failed. But he says, 'Don't worry. We still have three engines left. We're in no danger. All it means is that instead of taking about 5 hours to reach New York, it will take approximately 6 hours.' And the mathematicians are really charmed with this adventure, because nothing like this would ever happen back home, where all the transportation runs on the principle of antigravitational dark matter reverse polarization. Then a few hours later, another engine fails. And the captain says, 'Don't worry. We still have two engines left. All it means is that instead of taking 6 hours to reach New York, it will take us approximately 8 hours.' And the Alpha Centaurians have a few drinks and discuss this great story they'll have to tell all their friends. A few more hours go by, and the third engine fails, and the captain says, 'Don't worry, it just means instead of taking 8 hours to reach New York, it will take us 16 hours to reach our destination.' And one of the Alpha Centaurian abstract transcendental mathematicians turns to the other and says, 'I hope we don't have another engine failure, or we'll be up here forever.'

"That fourth engine is the tipping point."

"Is it your whole atmosphere that's heating up?" Sol asks me, "From the stratosphere right down to the ground?"

"Actually," says my atmosphere, "my upper layers are getting colder, while my lower ones are getting warmer."

"Then I don't think it's me ..." says Sol.

"Not to bring up a sore point, sweetheart, but you did boil away *my* oceans," says Venus.

"That was a little different," says Sol patiently.

"How different, Solly?" asks Venus. "Earth and I are neighbors. We're close to the same in size, density, and composition."

"But don't forget, you're closer to me."

"How can I forget, Solly-kins? It would be like forgetting the day you started frying the CO2 out of my rocks."

"It's called 'sublimating', not 'frying'," says Mercury, crisply.

"You try it sometime, darling. When your surface temperature hits 480° C (896° F), tell me if you care what it's called. Did you know I don't even have any oxygen left in my atmosphere? It all boiled away into outer space."

"You have an atmosphere?" says Mercury, his voice dripping with envy. "That must be marvelous. Mine got blown away by solar wind."

"I have an idea," says Sol, still grinning. "On Earth, one of the life forms has a day of rest they call Sunday. How about we declare a solar-system-wide day of rest? We'll call it HateOnTheSunDay. I'll take the day off myself - that is, as long as you all don't mind flying off into space and turning into balls of ice. Oh, no, wait a minute, I forgot - there's no such thing as a solar-system-wide day. Every celestial body has its own rhythm of days and nights, depending on how fast it's spinning around. And I have no days or nights at all, because I'm providing them for everyone else. I'm on duty all the time."

"All I know, Solly," says Venus, "is my atmosphere is 97% CO_2, and it feels like I'm wearing a fur coat in a hothouse."

"Do you think maybe if I'm especially well-behaved they'll give *me* an atmosphere? Then maybe my temperature wouldn't vary 1,130° F (630° C) every time I rotate!" says Mercury.

"Children! Children!" says Sol. "My surface temperature is 5,400° C (9,800° F). Do you hear me complaining? No, I'm too busy pulling off the crime of the century."

"Look, Sol," I say, "I'm not accusing you of anything ..."

"Good. Cause if the warming you're talking about was just caused by more sunlight, then wouldn't *all* the layers of your atmosphere …"

"But I gotta check out every angle."

"You do, huh?" says Sol. "Well, I gotta say I admire your dedication, kid. All right. So. Tilt, wobble and stretch."

"Obliquity, precession and eccentricity," insists Mercury.

"How about obliquity, precession, eccentricity, and shutting up, darling?" says Venus.

"Imagine our system as a huge carousel," Sol says to me, trying to ignore them. "I'm at the center. Instead of horses, we have planets. And instead of going up and down, you rotate around your posts. For example, Earth, you rotate every 24 hours. That's what causes your day and night: Half of you always being in daylight facing me, while the other half is in night facing an amusement park full of stars and planets."

"Listen, Sol, I love amusement parks …"

"Great! Now, it takes you a year to go around the carousel ..."

"... but I'm actually on the clock right now ..."

"Right. And I'm your big suspect."

"An amusement park!" says Venus, "Is that something you can have when you're capable of supporting life?"

"Now, early on," Sol says to me, "you got tilted."

"Bingo!" screeches the water flea from the Baltic Sea. "And while tilted, he could have flown into a rage, heated the environment, murdered the countess, framed Arrhenius, and buried the body in the garden by the stone bench."

Everyone stares at the flea like it was interstellar gas on an eccentric orbit around a brown dwarf exoplanet.

"Wha-at?! This is a mystery, right?" says the flea. "Just trying to help."

"Your seasons are caused by your tilt," Sol continues. "When your *north* pole tilts towards me, it's warmer up north. When your *south* pole tilts towards me, it's warmer down south."

"And why would he change his tilt?" screeches the water flea. "To confuse the authorities? First, they would think they were getting warmer when they looked down south. Then they would think they were getting warmer when ..."

"I don't change my tilt," I explain.

"*Au contraire*," says Venus, "as he orbits Sol, he maintains his alignment with his celestial north and south poles: fixed, unchanging points in the heavens."

"So," concludes Sol, "if he's tilted *towards* me when he's on one side of me, naturally when he gets around to the other side, since his alignment with the fixed stars hasn't changed, he'll be tilted *away* from me."

"*My* axis is straight up and down," says Mercury, "And my days and nights are equal all year round. I have no seasons to speak of. For me, it's a marvelous merry-go-round of no atmosphere, no tilt, no seasons, … and no hope." (Mercury tries valiantly to fight back a sniffle.)

"I don't have much tilt, either," says Venus, "and hardly any seasons."

"But you," says Sol to me, "you got tilt. You tilt towards the floor of the carousel ..."

"Better known in real life as the *ecliptic plane*," says Mercury.

"... twenty-some degrees."

"And just because of that, he gets seasons?!" says Venus. "It's not fair! Tilt. Seasons. Earth gets everything!"

"Maybe," the water flea suggests, "Earth is just getting more tilted, so his seasons are getting more extreme. That could explain all these natural disasters *Homo sapiens* is complaining about."

"Except for one thing," says Sol, "Earth's tilt has been *decreasing* for thousands of years. And it's going to keep decreasing for thousands of years to come."

"Oh."

"Earth's decreasing tilt should be making the seasons less extreme," says Sol. "And though you might think that milder seasons would favor warming, in the past they've actually favored the growth of ice sheets and glaciers."

"But wouldn't warmer winters mean less ice and snow?" asks the water flea.

"Not necessarily," says Sol. "You can get a blizzard when Mexican air meets Canadian air over North Dakota. If the Mexican air is warmer, it can hold more moisture. So warmer air may actually mean *more* snow. Then if the ice and snow melt later because of a milder summer, that increases the albedo and starts a feedback loop towards more and more cooling."

"This is so interesting! I love this stuff!" says the water flea.

"Me, too, Sol, genuinely, but … Unghh!" Suddenly someone sneaks up behind me and clobbers me with around 30 billion tons of CO2 per year.

When I wake up, the water flea is saying to Sol, "So you're saying the changes in the tilt and wobble of Earth's axis, and the stretch of Earth's orbit, should all be moving us towards a milder climate, and eventually an ice age sometime in the next 10,000 to 170,000 years?"

"Yep," says Sol.

"So," asks the water flea, "if someone is trying to pin that Environment job on you ..."

"It's a frame-up. I haven't gotten any brighter in the last 50 years. At least, that's what Venus tells me! Ha ha! Besides, when Earth does get more energy from me, *every* layer of his atmosphere gets warmer. When his *lower* layers get warmer and his *top* ones get colder, the way they are now, it means that Earth's own radiant heat is getting trapped in the bottom layers of his atmosphere and isn't reaching the higher ones."

"But who would try to frame you?" the water flea asks Sol. "Maybe this Guy Callendar …"

The *P. azotogensis* did say it was a *Homo sapiens* who suggested that Sol might be the perp. But why would *HS* want to incriminate the ultimate source of all life on the planet? I stare into the dark side of my sky, turning it over, trying to put it all together.

"Do you ever feel that you're lost in this … celestial sea of stars?" Venus asks, musingly. "Clusters, planets, comets, nebulæ, galaxies. Each one shining its light, great or small: hopeful flickering diamonds, bright yellow laughing sparkles, smoky smoldering rubies, dark, miserable violet blue sapphires. Or maybe … maybe we're all clear, flawless jewels, reflecting the shifting rainbow light of destiny's whim."

"Sounds about right." *Destiny's whim. Which, for me, I guess, at the moment, is an engineer-inventor named Guy Callendar.*

I put on my typical English workingman's gray woolen cloth cap from the early 20th century, with the large circular low crown attached to the stiff peak by a press stud.

X.

After several calendars suitable for guys, a number of guys suitable for calendars, a non-Jewish calendar, and one happy, carefree colander, I'm talking with "Ace" *Acetobacter* in an eel, pie and mash shop in East London.

"You're looking a bit bumfuzzled, guv'nor! Everything all right?" Ace asks, as it turns a bit of ethanol into acetic acid, adding a tang of vinegar to the briney smell of gelatinous eels.

"Somebody's been hitting me with 30 billion tons of carbon dioxide per year. Guess I'm a little dazed. But that's not important. I've got to find Guy Callendar right away."

"Guy Callendar? The famous climate scientist?"

"The same. I have reason to believe he may have conspired to burn The Environment and then pin the rap on a pal of mine. So you know where I can find this mug?"

"I know you can't. He's ..."

"Don't tell me. His wife accidentally poisoned him, he fell down the stairs and died of natural causes."

"He died in '64. Don't know about all the rest of it."

"Well, that's my job - to find out about 'all the rest of it'. Of course, he was jovial, loved by all, and had no enemies?"

"I wouldn't say 'jovial' exactly. He was a reserved, quiet, unassuming fellow. At the same time, he was a fighter."

"Aha! Plenty of mob guys in the fight game," I observe, "especially back in the early days. Maybe he got mixed up with the wrong crowd, refused to take a dive, stole the Meltese Dodo, and made some enemies in low places."

"What? He just fought for the idea that humans were heating the environment by increasing the concentration of CO2 in the atmosphere."

"Just like Arrhenius! Which got *him* in hot water with Knut Ångström. So maybe the Knut Ångström mob has a friendly scientific disagreement with Callendar and decides to increase the concentration of CO2 in *his* atmosphere - *permanently*!"

"Well," says Ace, "Ångström's experiments *were* one of the many reasons that scientists thought that increased CO2 wouldn't have the effect Callendar was predicting. But Ångström died in 1910, when Callendar was only about twelve."

"Aha! So in '64, when Callendar meets with his *unfortunate accident*, no one's going to point the finger at a guy who's been dead for … 54 years. The perfect crime!"

"Why, you're absolutely ..." Ace begins.

"Yeah, yeah," I interrupt. "You get a sense for these things after a while. I mean, think about it: Herschel tumbles to invisible heat and tips Fourier, who dopes out that my atmosphere's got the hots for me. Tyndall catches wise that it's primarily CO2 giving the air that invisible glow. By Callendar's time, Tyndall's tale has been corroborated by hundreds of sci-witnesses. So Ångström's gångstörs know beyond a reasonable doubt that increased atmospheric CO2 means increased warming. And of course they're intimately familiar with the Industrial Revolution and fossil fuels - burned by humans - releasing CO2.

"Put it all together, Callendar's got the winning hand. And yet, here's the Knut Ångström mob betting on the come, and cool as Copernicus with aces wired. Almost like *the fix was in*."

"You know, you've got a really sour, cynical attitude towards life. I like that."

"Thanks."

"However," Ace continues, "I don't think you're necessarily too bright. Callendar's opponents actually had some reasonable scientific objections to his idea. First, there was Ångström's experiment showing that decreasing CO2 in a test tube didn't actually decrease heat absorption that much. And, by the way, Ångström was an expert on radiant heat. It wasn't even Arrhenius' primary interest. And Callendar was just a talented amateur when it came to climate."

"Aha! Just as I suspected! The Ångström mob has the real dope, and they're setting Callendar up for a fall. An innocent amateur who thinks he knows his way around a hypothesis. He sticks his statistics out and - bam! - they conk him with a tall, cool test tube of CO2. Next thing he knows, his little theorem has lost its conclusion - *permanently*."

"Well … actually," says Ace, "it turned out the expert was wrong and the amateur was right. Ångström's measurements were inaccurate. Modern tests show a decrease in absorption two and a half times what Ångström reported. Ångström also assumed that a change in absorption of, say, one percent, would be insignificant. In reality, because of positive feedbacks, a one percent change could bring massive disruptions in climate.

"Most important, though, a major premise of Ångström's experiment was wrong. He thought of the atmosphere as a single mass. Actually, the atmosphere is layered, and heat escapes at the top layer, where it's very cold, very low pressure, and there is almost no water vapor. It turns out things work a lot differently up there than in a nice warm test tube at sea level in a laboratory."

"Aha! So Ångström is the fall guy and Callendar is the perp! I had a funny feeling! Callendar lets Ångström think his little test tube experiment will predict what the climate will do, and then, when Ångström is feeling all comfy – bam! – Callendar wallops him with the completely unexpected behavior of CO2 in the dry, frigid top layer of my atmosphere. I bet Ångström never saw it coming. Especially since CO2 is a totally invisible, odorless gas."

"Ye-ah. Something like that. Also, in 1938, when Callendar first presented his idea, the instruments they had to measure the absorption bands of CO2 and water vapor – which precise wavelengths of radiant heat each gas would absorb – showed that the two overlapped so much that increasing CO2 simply wouldn't make much difference: All the wavelengths that CO2 could affect were already being taken out by water vapor. Or so they thought."

"But in reality ..."

"In reality, especially in the upper atmosphere where it really matters, modern measurements show distinctly different absorption bands."

"Clever! And nearly foolproof! In 1910, Callendar bops Ångström. Who's going to think a twelve year old English kid popped a 53 year old Swedish physicist, right? Especially since Ångström is probably married, eats and uses stairways, which puts him in a high risk category. After icing Ångström, Callendar lays low for 28 years, then - bam! - he publishes his hypothesis, *knowing* it is 1938, so only measuring instruments *from* 1938 will be available. Now all he has to do is wait, in full confidence that at some point in the future, measurements *will be modern*! Ångström never had a chance."

"Amazing. I have absolutely no idea what you're talking about. I do know, however, that in 1938 scientists weren't even sure that CO2 really was rising. The scientific community generally believed it was impossible to accurately measure global levels of CO2. It seemed to vary too much by time and place. For instance, they measured higher levels near cow pastures and flocks of sheep and lower ones in London during a bank holiday."

"Aha! So Callendar could have measured levels during a London bank holiday when he was twelve, waited eighteen years, and then measured levels again in a cow pasture, making it appear that levels had risen!"

"Yes! That's right! I never thought of that, because I'm not a complete moron!" Ace says, with perhaps a hint of sarcasm that could peel the fusion crust off a meteorite. "What Callendar actually did, however, was compile measurements of temperatures and CO2 concentrations from many different locations going back a hundred years. And he determined that, over that time, atmospheric CO2 had gone up about ten percent. Most importantly, in 1900 it was somewhere between 274 to 292 parts per million by volume (ppmv), and by 1938, it had risen to 289 to 310 ppmv. And he concluded that the resulting 'sky radiation' (downward infrared radiation) would be enough to cause the observed increase in surface temperature."

"Hmm. But is Callendar right and the entire rest of the scientific community wrong? Or has Callendar stolen the Meltese Dodo from Ångström and tried to cover up his crime by raising the temperature of Europe to the point where Swedes will begin to express personal feelings in public, to non-family members? In the pandemonium that would ensue, Callendar could escape ..."

"I'll just pretend you're not saying anything. It turned out Callendar was probably right about CO2 levels. When widely-accepted measurements emerged in the early 50's (thanks to pioneering work by Charles David "Dave" Keeling at the Scripps Institution of Oceanography) the global level was 310 ppmv. Right in line with Callendar's estimates."

"Aha! So Callendar lets Ångström *think* that no one can tell whether CO2 is rising or not, and then, when Ångström dies - bam! - Keeling waltzes in forty years later with widely-accepted measurements that just happen to back up Callendar's story. Almost like *they planned the whole thing*."

"Wow! That's amazing-"

"It's nothing, really."

"-ly stupid. There was still an objection to Callendar's claim, though."

"Aha!"

"Aha! Aha! Aha!" Ace starts screaming, flailing its tiny flagella, and writhing dramatically around the jellied eels.

"You okay?" I ask.

"Oh, yes, absolutely wonderful. No problem at all. Could you never say 'aha' again in my presence? Thank you very kindly. You see, the oceans contain fifty times as much CO2 as the atmosphere, so most scientists assumed the oceans would continue to absorb the bulk of the man-made CO2. The best estimate was that the average molecule of CO2 would get absorbed by the oceans within 10 years, and then swept to the bottom and deposited there, never to rise again."

"A ..." I catch myself quickly, "… choo! Just as I suspected, Ångström gave Callendar enough rope to hang himself, letting him *think* CO2 levels would continue to rise. Then, just when Callendar is starting to relax, the oceans drop by with *a little surprise*. And now someone's going to the bottom, and it ain't Ångström! Callendar probably never knew what hit him."

"Actually, no, once again, the scientific establishment turned out to be wrong, and Callendar turned out to be right. Radiocarbon dating of CO2 in ocean water revealed that only a small proportion of it comes from burning ancient coal and oil. Most of it is much newer, meaning it doesn't come from burning fossil fuels. So the oceans *aren't* absorbing most of the CO2 we create, aha aha aha just as you had no freaking idea. What most scientists hadn't understood, and what Roger Revelle at Scripps explained, is that the oceans 'buffer' CO2 as is, re-emit ninety percent of what they absorb - aha aha aha just as you were completely clueless about.

“And - consistent with the slow absorption of CO2 by the oceans - Keeling's measurements revealed a predictable straight-line rise in atmospheric CO2 levels year after year. (Though the straight line was overlaid by regular daily and seasonal variations, and care had to be taken to ensure that measurements weren't contaminated by local emissions - all the things that had confounded previous researchers.) The graph of that steady rise came to be known as the 'Keeling curve': a zig-zag where each year's zig is a little higher than the previous one, and each year's zag is not quite as low, aha aha aha just as you never ever suspected and please don't say you did, thank you, good-bye.”

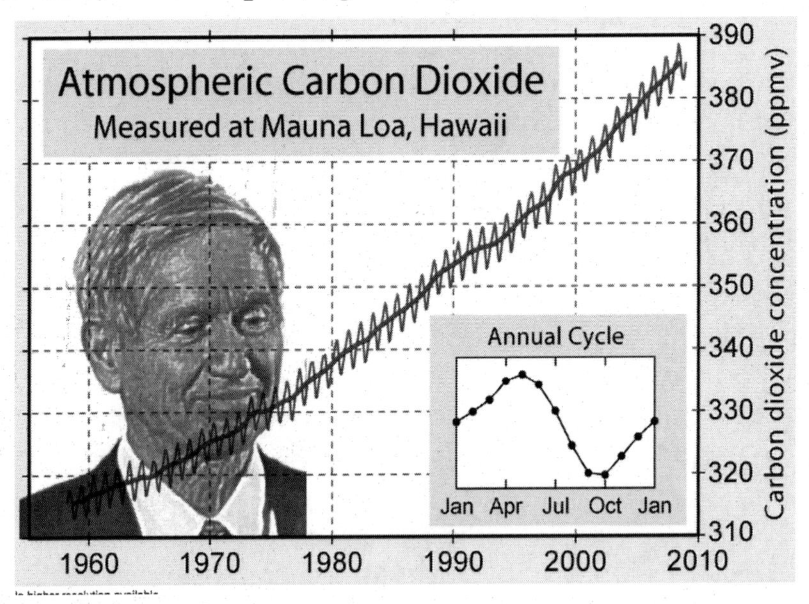

XI.

Back at the Baltic, I find *Homo sapiens* hopelessly tangled in the fishing net. I free her, get her on the boat, dry her off. She wants to try fishing again, this time with a spear gun, but I've had enough.

* * *

Homo sapiens sits in my office, looking cool as an interstellar ice simulation experiment in an astrophysics laboratory.

"So, why make things hot for me?" I want to know. "What's the grift?"

Homo sapiens looks at me like I've got three poles. "I don't know what you're talking about."

"Don't try to con me. Believe me, doll, I have pursued every other explanation, no matter how cockamamie it might seem, because I didn't want to believe it was you. But it is. Ever since the Industrial Revolution, you've been burning more and more fossil fuel, dumping more and more CO2 into my atmosphere. That traps heat. Basic nineteenth century science. Yet you come to me like you don't know who's putting the heat on me."

"On you? Wait a minute. Are you saying … you're The Environment?"

"That's right, doll. And The Extinctor. I wear a lot of hats."

"So you were investigating yourself? I don't get it."

"It's true, you really don't. Look, my oceans had been packing heat since the 1970s. In a thousand places all over me, spring was coming earlier, glaciers were losing ice, plants and animals from the south were migrating north. Any one of these things would have been no big deal. But taken together, I knew they meant one thing: I had a fever. But I didn't know why.

"When you waltzed in and told me your story, right away I knew you had to be desperate or insane, or both. I mean, what species in its right mind goes up against The Environment? And when you told me The Environment had sent you that note about the Meltese Dodo …"

"But if you're The Environment, you must have known about that already!" objects *Homo sapiens*. "It would have been *you* that sent the note."

"You know," I explain, "when you walk, I bet there's a thousand little messages going out every second, moving twenty different muscles, balancing, speeding up, slowing down. And most of it, you're completely unaware of. In fact, a lot of it, you wouldn't understand if it was explained to you. Plus, ninety-nine percent of what you do, you probably forget. I'm the same way. I may have sent you that note, but I wouldn't necessarily know it or remember it.

"Still, I knew if I *did* send that note, there had to be a reason. So I'm thinking – *Meltese Dodo* – I had never heard of such a thing. And neither had anybody else I talked to.

"At first, 'Meltese' reminded me of the grilled cheese sandwich who walks into a bar. And the bartender says, 'I'm sorry, sir, we don't serve food here.' So I was really hoping the whole thing was just a bad joke.

"But then I remembered the climate modeler, the meteorologist and the skeptic who are viewing the stuffed dodo at the British Museum, and the curator tells them that the dodo is extinct. So the climate modeler says, 'I'm going to assume that dodos are extinct'. And the meteorologist says, 'All we really know is that this particular dodo is extinct, for now.' And the skeptic rolls his eyes and says, 'Gentlemen! Please! All we really know is that in a building purporting to be the British Museum there exists a stuffed animal which a supposed curator claims to be a dodo, one side of which appears to be extinct'.

"That's when I realized I had to look at this thing from all angles before I made a decision.

"The signs were everywhere: Jellyfish - Mauve Stingers - usually found in African waters, showing up by the millions in the Mediterranean. Blue-green algae blooms and zebra mussel infestations in the Great Lakes. Zooplankton from Spain migrating to Sweden, while their cold-water relatives head still farther north. Warm water species like the fishhook water flea increasing in the Baltic Sea off Sweden and Finland.

"Meanwhile, I learned that CO2 has been increasing steadily at least since the 1950's, when Dave Keeling developed techniques for measuring it precisely. Now, where do you think all that CO2 could be coming from?"

"But hasn't CO2 has increased before, many times, going back millions of years, before I was even born? I obviously wasn't responsible for those. What makes you so sure it's me this time?"

"Right. It's like the dame they found standing over her boyfriend's body with a smoking gun, a bullet in him that matched the gun, gunshot residue on her sleeve and hand, and her fingerprint on the trigger. And the dame's mouthpiece says, very logically, 'Look, people get killed every day. Obviously, my client is not committing all these murders. And that makes me very doubtful that she committed this one.' And when she comes up for trial, the judge says if she ain't guilty of every murder, then she never killed anybody at all. So they let her go."

"Really?" says *Homo sapiens*, hopefully.

"Well ... Actually, they fried her. You see, she killed her boyfriend."

HS starts to speak, but I hold my palm out. "No, sweetheart. You burned the fossil fuel and you're going over for it. The smoking gun is internal combustion. The matching bullet is Keeling's curve. The gunshot residue is the concentration of CO2 near urban areas and factories. The fingerprint is the pattern of warming first predicted by Arrhenius, with more warming towards the poles and at higher altitudes. And the Meltese Dodo is you."

"No! Please! I … I love you!" says *Homo sapiens*, rather convincingly.

"I got feelings for you, too, doll. But if I don't send you over, I'll regret it. Maybe not today. Maybe not tomorrow, but perhaps within decades, and almost certainly by the year 2100."

"All right, all right. I admit it. I lied to you. But it's only because I wanted to get The Environment off my back so that I could stay with you. Because I love you. Is that so wrong?"

"Not wrong, sweetheart. Just a little late. We've passed my tipping point."

As the years pass, with increasing frequency, my floods drown the species; my heat waves, cold snaps, growing deserts and dust storms starve the species; my rising oceans and tsunamis drive it from its homes; my droughts and ice storms destroy crops; my hurricanes and typhoons wreck villages and cities; my viruses kill young and old; my famines, oil shortages and water shortages bring war; and always I elude capture.

"Help! Save me!" cries *HS*.

"You had plenty of chances to do that yourself. And not only did you refuse to save *yourself*: You caused tens of thousands of extinctions of *other species* every year, decade after decade. These are my species, and I'm supposed to do something about it. I may not enjoy it, but that doesn't matter. The Earth, The Environment, The Extinctor - whatever you want to call me - is supposed to do something about it. If I let you get away with it, it would be bad all around - bad for me, and bad for every planet everywhere."

"We could run away together."

"Where to, darling? No, I'm sending you over. Maybe you'll get off with near extinction. With sane behavior, you could re-establish yourself as a species. If you do, I'll be waiting for you. And if not … I'll always remember you."

* * *

After they take the species away, I put my feet up on the desk and take out *The Maltese Falcon*. But I end up just closing my eyes and letting a meteor shower of images flash across my inner space. This has been a once-in-a-tilt-wobble-and-stretch experience. Hopefully.

I still seem to have that fever. But give me a couple of millennia. It'll pass.

Image Attribution/Copyright:

Chapter I.

Chapter II

Two images in this chapter incorporate and adapt photos:

Image of earth standing looking up at the facade St. Etienne Cathedral in Auxerre incorporates and adapts a photo on fr.wikipedia.com_by Christophe Finot

(http://commons.wikimedia.org/wiki/File:Auxerre_-_Cathedrale_Saint-Etienne_-_20.jpg)

The following image, of The Earth reading, incorporates and adapts a photo on fr.wikipedia.com by Christophe Finot (http://commons.wikimedia.org/wiki/File:Auxerre_-_Cathedrale_Saint-Etienne_-_04.jpg)

Chapters III and IV

(Some images incorporate public domain images from fr.wikipedia.com.)

Chapter V

Hare is adapted from a public domain sketch created by Albrecht Durer in 1502: https://en.wikipedia.org/wiki/Young_Hare

Chapter VI

(Some images incorporate public domain images from en.wikipedia.com.)

Chapter VII

The second figure incorporates and adapts a photo of eagles mating by Dan Pacamo:

http://en.wikipedia.org/wiki/Bald_eagle#/media/File:Dan_Pancamo_Baytown_Bald_Eagles_Fall_2010-1.jpg

Chapter VIII

(Some images incorporate public domain images from en.wikipedia.com.)

Chapter IX

Chapter X

Chapter XI